KISS THE MOONLIGHT

Barbara Cartland, the celebrated novelist, playwright, lecturer, political and television personality, has now written over 200 books. She has written a number of historical books and several autobiographical ones, including a biography of her brother, Ronald Cartland, who was the first Member of Parliament to be killed in the war. The preface was written by Sir Winston Churchill.

In private life, Barbara Cartland is a Dame of Grace of St. John of Jerusalem, and one of the first women, after a thousand years, to be admitted to the Chapter General. Chairman of the St. John Council for Hertfordshire, she has served in the St. John Ambulance Brigade for thirty-five years.

Barbara Cartland has fought for better conditions and salaries for midwives and nurses, and, as President of the Hertfordshire Branch of the Royal College of Midwives, she has been invested with the first Badge of Office ever given in Great Britain, which was subscribed to by the midwives themselves. She has also championed the cause of old people and founded the first Romany Gypsy Camp in the world. It was christened 'Barbaraville' by the gypsies.

Barbara Cartland is deeply interested in Vitamin Therapy and is President of the National Association for Health.

By the same author in Pan Books

The Dangerous Dandy
The Ruthless Rake
The Bored Bridegroom
The Penniless Peer
The Cruel Count
The Castle of Fear
A Very Naughty Angel
Call of the Heart
The Frightened Bride
The Flame is Love
Say Yes, Samantha
As Eagles Fly
An Arrow of Love
A Gamble with Hearts
A Kiss for the King
A Frame of Dreams
Moon Over Eden
Fragrant Flower
The Golden Illusion
No Time for Love
The Husband Hunters
The Slaves of Love
Passions in the Sand
An Angel in Hell
The Incredible Honeymoon
The Dream and the Glory
Conquered by Love
Love Locked In

For other titles by Barbara Cartland,
please see page 158

BARBARA CARTLAND

KISS THE MOONLIGHT

A Pan Original
Pan Books London and Sydney

First published 1977 by Pan Books Ltd,
Cavaye Place, London SW10 9PG
© Cartland Promotions 1977
ISBN 0 330 25088 4
Printed and bound in Great Britain by
Hazell Watson & Viney Ltd, Aylesbury, Bucks

This book is sold subject to the condition that it
shall not, by way of trade or otherwise, be lent, re-sold,
hired out or otherwise circulated without the publisher's prior
consent in any form of binding or cover other than that in which
it is published and without a similar condition including this
condition being imposed on the subsequent purchaser

Dedicated to the ex-Ambassador to the Court of St. James, His Excellency General Nicholas Broumas and his lovely wife, Clary, whose warmth, generosity and affection to my son and me was everything that we had hoped to find in Greece.

Author's note

In 1899 the French archaeologists moved the village of Delphi and discovered underneath it the wonders of the bronze Charioteer, the altar of Athena and many statues and friezes of great beauty.

I visited Delphi in 1976 and found that the Shrine to Apollo had a strange, ecstatic serenity which is indescribable. The Shining Cliffs, rising protectively behind the broken columns, look over the loveliest view in Greece.

The Temple of Athena, surrounded by olive trees, has a mystic charm which is different from any other Temple I have visited.

In 1837 an historian wrote that the whole of Greece was infested with brigands whom the Bavarian Government were unable to hold in check. This was one of the causes of the revolution of 1862 which drove King Otho from his throne.

Chapter One
1852

Athena came out of her bed-room window onto the balcony to stand looking at the vista in front of her.

Every time she saw a view in Greece she thought it more beautiful than it had been a moment before, and yet it seemed impossible that anything could be lovelier than the blue sea of the Gulf of Corinth.

The setting sun turned the coast-line to gold until in the distance it became purple merging to misty grey where it met the sky.

Athena knew that behind the Palace the sun would be throwing fantastic shadows on the mountains against which the Summer Palace of the Princes of Parnassus gleamed like a pearl.

Everything, she felt, had a mystery and a wonder about it that she had never envisaged, even though she had been sure that Greece would in fact be even more breathtaking than her wildest dreams.

All her life she had longed to come to Greece.

Ever since she had been a small child her grandmother, the Dowager Marchioness, had regaled her with stories of the Greek gods and goddesses; of Pan who blew his pipes under the olive trees, and of Zeus who sat in all his majesty on the summit of Mount Olympus.

While other children had read the story of Cinderella, of Hansel and Gretel, Athena had read of the adoration in which her namesake was held.

Not that in England anyone thought of her as Athena.

To her family she was Mary Emmeline, and to the outside world she was Lady Mary Emmeline Athena Wade, daughter of the 4th Marquess of Wadebridge, and as such an important social figure.

The sun sank a little lower and now the whole sea was suddenly shimmering with glittering gold and the light from it combined with the translucence of the sky seemed almost blinding.

She could remember her grandmother saying: "The Greeks were never tired of describing the appearance of light. They loved the glitter of moist things, of stones and sand washed by the sea, of fish churning in the nets, and their Temples glowed like pillars of light."

"It is what I feel," Athena thought.

She compared the sunset with this morning when she had risen very early to see "the rosy fingered dawn" and imagined that the whole body of Apollo was pouring across the sky, flashing with a million points of light, healing everything he touched and defying the powers of darkness.

Apollo was very real to her for, as her grandmother had explained, he was not only the sun but the moon, the planets, the Milky Way, and the faintest stars.

"He is the sparkle on the waves," the Dowager Marchioness had said, "the gleam in one's eyes, the strange glimmer of fields on darkest nights."

Athena had remembered the lines from Homer, "Make the sky clear and grant us to see with our eyes."

She had read all she could find of the Greek poets who wrote of the light. She found herself often murmuring the lines from Pindar's ode –

> "We are all shadows, but when the shining comes
>   from the hands of the gods,
> Then the heavenly light falls on men."

Would the heavenly light ever fall on her, she wondered; and if it did, what would she feel?

The setting sun carried a prayer from her heart, but Athena was aware that time was passing and she would be expected downstairs for dinner.

She turned from the balcony, crossed her bed-room floor and stepped onto the landing at the top of the stairs.

Again there was beauty to make her draw in her breath – the curve of the stone staircase, the mosaics against the white walls, the golden light coming through the long windows through which she could see the brilliant flowers which filled the green garden.

She paused instinctively because it was so beautiful, and as she did so she heard a man's voice below say in Greek:

"Do you mean to tell me that you have brought me no news of His Highness?"

Athena knew who was speaking. It was the deep, rather hoarse voice of the Prince's Comptroller, Colonel Stefanatis.

"No, Sir," a younger voice replied. "I have been to all the places you instructed me, but there was no sign of His Highness."

There was a pause before the Colonel said:

"You called at Madame Helena's Villa?"

"Yes, Sir. She left a week ago and the servants have no idea where she has gone."

There was another pause which Athena felt was somehow pregnant with meaning. Then the Colonel said as if he spoke to himself:

"It is an impossible situation – impossible!"

Suddenly he said sharply:

"You had better rest, Captain. I shall require you to start out again to-morrow morning."

"Very good, Sir."

Athena heard the young officer's heels click as he drew himself to attention and he walked away, his spurs jingling as he moved across the marble floor.

With difficulty she forced herself to descend the stairs slowly and in an unconcerned manner, as if she had not overheard what had been said.

But if the Colonel thought the situation was impossible, to her it was incredible.

She had come to Greece from England because it had

been arranged by her grandmother that she should marry Prince Yiorgos of Parnassus.

It was the result of negotiations with which the Dowager Marchioness had been concerned for nearly two years.

Although Xenia Parnassus was only a distant relative of the Prince, the ties of family and the blood of her ancestors pulsated in her veins and never let her rest.

Extremely beautiful she had taken English Society by storm from the moment the 3rd Marquess of Wadebridge searching for Grecian antiquities had brought back with him not only a collection of vases, statues and urns, but also a wife.

The Greeks were extremely profligate with their treasures and, as Athena had learnt in Athens, not particularly interested in what they called "Ruins".

From the time that Lord Elgin had committed what Lord Byron had raged over as "vandalism" in shipping the Acropolis Marbles to England, dozens of aristocrats with a yearning for culture had journeyed to Greece to see what they too could pillage from the past.

*"Dull is the eye that will not weep to see
Thy walls defaced, thy mouldering shrines removed."*

Lord Byron had thundered, but no-one listened.

Country houses in England and museums all over Europe were packed with the spoils from Greece.

Xenia Parnassus, once she had become the Marchioness of Wadebridge, had never returned to her own country.

She had however presented her adoring husband with six extremely good-looking children, although none of them had measured up to her idealised standard of beauty until her grandchild, Athena had arrived.

The Marchioness had known when she first saw the baby that it was what she had always wanted; a child who resembled the goddess who meant more to her than all the saints in the Church calendar.

"I insist that she is given the name of Athena," she said firmly.

The family protested: the Wades had never gone in for fancy names and the Marquess's first daughter must be christened Mary, as was traditional, then Emmeline after a famous ancestor whose portraits hung on the walls at Wadebridge Castle.

It had taken a great deal of persistence for the Marchioness to get her way but finally her granddaughter had been christened Mary Emmeline Athena. The third name however was never used except by the Dowager Marchioness and her granddaughter herself.

"Of course I want to be called Athena, Grandmama," she had said when she was nine years old. "It is a pretty name, and I think the name Mary is dull and Emmeline is ugly."

She wrinkled her small nose, which even when she was a baby had the straightness of the statues which the Dowager Marchioness took her to see in the British Museum.

From then on the goddess Athena was as real to her as a member of her own family.

The Dowager Marchioness told her of Athena the Warrior shaking her spear; of Athena the companion, almost the lover; of Athena of the household presiding over the young weavers – the goddess of all things fair who gazed down on her charges with maternal solicitude.

Most important of all there was Athena, the Virgin, immaculate and all powerful, resolved to protect the chastity of her city, who was also Athena, goddess of love.

"It was she to whom the women prayed when they wished for children," the Dowager Marchioness explained.

"And she brought them love?" Athena asked.

"Because they loved and were loved they had beautiful children – beautiful, both in body and in soul," the Dowager Marchioness replied.

The rest of the family found the Dowager Marchioness as she grew older somewhat of a bore with her predilection for Greece and her endless stories of the ancient gods.

But to Athena they were always absorbing, always exciting.

It therefore seemed quite natural when as she reached eighteen her grandmother told her that her marriage had been arranged with the Prince of Parnassus and she would journey to Greece to meet him.

Vaguely she had thought from the various things her grandmother had said that this had been intended for some time and was why the Dowager Marchioness continually extolled the virtues and the charms of a young man she had never seen.

"He is strong and handsome; a good Ruler and a man whom his people trust," the Dowager Marchioness said positively.

Because he was Greek, Athena was perfectly prepared to believe that he was all these things.

But here she was in the Prince's Palace having been sent out to meet him and knowing that inevitably the story would end with wedding-bells – but there was no Prince.

It was perhaps, Athena thought, her Aunt's fault that he had not been waiting as they had expected on the Quay when the ship which had carried them from the Port of Germeno had docked in the small harbour of Mikis.

He had written a charming letter to her Aunt, Lady Beatrice Wade, saying he was unfortunately unable to meet them in Athens but would be waiting to greet them at his Summer Palace as soon as they wished to join him.

It had been at first planned that they should stay in Athens after their arrival from England for at least three weeks.

There were many members of the family for them to meet and King Otho asked that the future bride of the Ruler of one of the States should be presented to the Court.

Greece after winning her independence had later become a Kingdom in 1844 and King Otho, although he was a

Bavarian, had shown himself a little more interested in the people over whom he ruled but he was extremely unpopular.

But even King Otho, Athena thought, could not at this moment conjure up a Prince who had mysteriously disappeared at the moment he should be meeting his future bride.

Lady Beatrice had quite a lot to say on the subject when they were alone.

"I cannot understand it, Mary," she said sharply. "And I cannot believe that your father would consider it anything less than an insult that the Prince should not be here to greet you."

"He obviously expected us to stay longer in Athens," Athena answered.

"I sent a messenger ahead of us," Lady Beatrice replied, "and quite frankly I do not believe a word of the story that he is visiting some obscure part of his territory where they cannot get into communication with him."

"Then where else can he be?" Athena asked a little helplessly.

If it was not an insult, it was hardly an encouraging welcome for a bride who had come all the way from England to meet her bridegroom.

As she spoke, however, she looked out to sea.

She had learnt on arrival in Athens that the Prince wore a beard, and when she seemed surprised she had been told it was because he had served in the Greek Navy and like most Greeks was more at home on the sea than he was on the land.

Perhaps he had sailed to the opposite shores, Athena told herself, or even through the narrow Straits forming the western exit of the Gulf into the Ionian Sea.

There he could have visited some of the many islands and perhaps forgotten who would be waiting for him on his return to the Palace.

Yet however much one explained it away it was still a depressing thought, and now three days had passed since she and her Aunt had arrived and there was still no sign of the Prince.

The conversation she had heard from the landing offered an explanation she had not suspected previously.

Who was Madame Helena?

Athena had been brought up in the country and was very ignorant of the intrigues and loose behaviour of the social world; but she could not have read Greek mythology without realising that love had pre-occupied the gods and they had been continually enraptured by beautiful women.

For the first time since Athena had set out from England she questioned whether her marriage was likely to be a happy one.

She had been so swept away by all her grandmother had told her, by the stories which had coloured her youth and by her own instinctive yearnings for romance, that until now she had not really considered the Prince as a man.

He had been a mythical figure as attractive, and in a way as awe-inspiring, as one of the gods themselves.

But she had not envisaged him as a human being, a man to whom she would belong, a man with the desires and emotions of other men.

Now suddenly, as if she awoke from a dream, Athena realised that the Prince was flesh and blood, and never having seen her how could he be interested in her as she had been interested in him primarily because he was Greek?

To him there was nothing particularly romantic and certainly nothing mysterious or ethereal about her being English.

He would not have invested her with the mystery which to her surrounded the gods, and indeed he might dislike the very thought of her as his wife.

It was almost as if Athena had been drenched with cold water when she least expected it.

There had been a dream-like quality about the whole arrangement, the voyage from England, her arrival in Athens and most of all her first sight of the Palace.

Never had she believed anything could look so exquisite or that the mountains behind it could be so impressive.

She knew they were part of the Parnassus Range which extended north-west from the borders of Attica rising between the Boeotian plain and the sparsely inhabited northern shores of the Gulf of Corinth, the whole region rich in mythology and history.

Further to the east lay the rugged slopes of Mount Kitheron which was associated with the haunts of Pan and his goat-like satyrs and the sacred Mount Helicon where the nine Muses dwelt.

Far to the north in the centre of Greece stretched the mountain range which held as its highest peak the sacred Mount Olympus from where the gods themselves had once ruled.

Lady Beatrice was not concerned with mountains.

"As I have already told you, Mary," she said insistently, "this is the Summer Palace of the Princes of Parnassus. I believe their main Palace which is near Lividia is far more impressive, although sadly in need of repair."

There was a note in her Aunt's voice which told Athena all too clearly why she was accentuating the fact at this particular moment.

The whole reason that the marriage had been arranged, and her grandmother had not deceived her on this score, was that the Prince of Parnassus was in need of money.

The centuries of oppression under Turkish rule and the protracted struggle for freedom had left the country poverty-stricken and had taken its toll of what had once been a rich and proud family.

The obvious course for the Prince was to marry a rich wife, and that was where the Dowager Marchioness had played her trump card in the shape of Athena.

"When I was young," she said to her granddaughter, "it would have been deemed impossible for the head of our family to marry anyone who was not a Royal; but times have changed and the Wadebridges are one of the oldest and most important families in England."

"Yes, Grandmama," Athena had agreed dutifully.

"What is more," the Dowager Marchioness continued, "you are singularly fortunate in that you were left so much money by your godmother."

She had smiled in a way which was almost mischievous.

"I must take the credit for that, Athena, because your father and mother were very much against giving you an American godmother!"

Athena had laughed.

"So it was you who chose such a good fairy for me?"

"She indeed proved to be that," the Dowager Marchioness replied, "but who would have imagined that even though she had no children she would have made you her sole heiress?"

"Who indeed!"

"Money carries with it a great deal of responsibility, as I have always told you," the Dowager Marchioness went on, "and that is why, Athena, I can imagine nowhere where your fortune could be better spent than in Greece."

Athena had agreed with her, and it had seemed, until this moment, almost as if she was marrying a country rather than a man.

When she reached the hall the Colonel had moved into the Salon.

Before she joined him Athena tried to compose herself, knowing she must not let him realise she had overheard and understood his conversation with the young Captain.

She had not let the Prince's Comptroller know she could speak Greek. Her grandmother had been most insistent that she should speak the language ever since she was a child and she had hoped it might prove a delightful surprise to the Prince.

The members of the Prince's household automatically

spoke in English to answer their Master's questions and Lady Beatrice had no knowledge of any language other than her own and French.

"Perhaps it is a good thing they do not realise I understand everything that is said," Athena told herself.

Then she was afraid of what else she might discover.

She found it difficult at dinner to listen to the conversation between her Aunt and the Colonel or to answer the conventional, stiffly polite comments of the other officers who were present.

The Prince's mother was staying in the Palace, but she was in ill-health and invariably, Athena found, retired to bed before dinner.

She was a shy person which made her appear somewhat stiff in her manner to strangers, and Athena had felt ever since she arrived somewhat uncomfortable in her presence.

But now she wondered if it was because the Princess was not in fact pleased to accept her as a daughter-in-law.

"I am sure she would have wanted her son to marry a Greek," Athena told herself and wondered if the rest of the Parnassus family were prepared to swallow her like a nasty medicine only because she was rich.

It was a discouraging thought and remembering the people she had met in Athens and her reception at Court she recalled the somewhat searching looks they had given her.

Had this been because they were wondering why as she was so rich she should wish to marry a Greek Prince, unless it was for his title?

This idea was almost as much of a shock as the thought that the Prince might not be interested in her as a woman.

"How could they think such a thing?" Athena asked herself indignantly.

Yet it was, she admitted, the obvious explanation they would put upon her acceptance of a man she had never seen.

The whole marriage which up to now had been invested with a strange unearthly magic became something quite different.

Quite suddenly she felt horrified at everything that was happening.

How, she wondered wildly, had she ever been persuaded into setting out on a voyage to meet a man to whom she could mean nothing and who in fact could mean nothing to her.

Yet, because her grandmother had invested Greece with a splendour and a glory that was sacred she had accepted the suggestion of marriage almost as if it had been a gift from the gods.

"I must have been mad!" Athena thought.

Then she realised that while she had been thinking dinner had come to an end and she had not in fact heard one word of what had been said to her since about half-way through the meal.

Her Aunt led the way into the Salon.

"You seem a little distant this evening, Mary," she said. "The Colonel asked you the same question three times before you answered him."

"I am sorry, Aunt Beatrice, I think perhaps I am a little tired."

"It is the hot sun. You are not used to it," Lady Beatrice said. "As the Prince will doubtless be arriving shortly and I want you to look your best, it would be wise to go to bed and have a good night's rest."

"Yes, of course, Aunt Beatrice, I will do that."

Lady Beatrice glanced towards the door before she said in a low voice:

"The Colonel tells me they are still having difficulty in getting in touch with the Prince, but he is certain that His Highness will be here to-morrow. Nevertheless I am considering whether we should return to Athens. This waiting is extremely embarrassing."

"Perhaps we should have remained in the City the three

weeks they expected us to stay," Athena suggested.

"That is what we should have done," Lady Beatrice agreed, "but it is too late to think of it now. Everything has been planned by Mama and I am afraid I accepted her arrangements without questioning them. It was stupid of me."

For her Aunt to admit that she was at fault meant, Athena knew quite well, that she was extremely perturbed.

Because she herself felt so worried at the Prince's non-appearance, she felt it would not make the situation any better to discuss it.

"Do not worry, Aunt Beatrice," she said, "I am sure it will be all right. And it is so lovely here."

"It is quite an intolerable situation!" Lady Beatrice replied. "I must say I have always believed that the Greeks had good manners – until now!"

"The people we met in Athens were certainly very polite," Athena remarked.

"They all spoke most warmly of His Highness," Lady Beatrice said.

"Yes, indeed," Athena agreed.

But to herself she was wondering exactly what thoughts and intentions had lain beneath the complimentary manner in which they had talked about the Prince.

Had they been glad that he should have the money he urgently needed for his people?

The Parnassus country was, Athena knew, quite a large territory, stretching east of the mountains and being only partly productively fertile.

Travelling to Greece in one of its country's steam-ships, Athena had imagined herself riding over the land beside the Prince, deciding how they would improve the lot of the poorest, perhaps building better ports for the fishermen and raising the standard of education.

Now she suddenly felt uncertain and afraid.

Supposing he wished to do none of those things with her? Suppose Madame Helena, whoever she might be, should have his complete confidence and companionship?

She said good-night to her Aunt and retired to her own room before the Colonel and the other gentlemen came from the Dining-Room into the Salon.

When she was undressed she dismissed the maid who had waited on her and walked out onto the balcony to gaze once again on the sea.

Dusk was falling and there was the last glimmer of gold and crimson on the horizon. The stars were coming out in the velvet darkness over-head.

There was no wind, and although the great heat of the day had gone it was still warm.

She leaned over the balcony, her arms on the cool stone, and stared into the darkness.

"Why am I here?" she asked herself. "Why have I allowed myself to come to a place where I am not wanted as a person, but only as the purveyor of wealth?"

The idea horrified her.

Always she had been very conscious of herself as a person.

"Know thyself," one of the Seven Sages had said, and she tried to follow it because she knew it was the foundation of Greek thought to be honest and to understand her own feelings.

Looking back she knew she had been bemused as a child would be with fairy-stories. She had not faced reality. She had just let herself drift into a day-dream that had seemed real simply because she had wanted it to be.

Now she had woken up.

"What can I do?"

The question was insistent, almost as if someone had asked it aloud, and Athena shivered.

She saw how easily she had been manipulated by her grandmother into accepting the idea of marriage and she saw only too clearly that she was now involved almost to the point of no return.

"Supposing I hate the Prince and he hates me?" she asked herself. "What can I do about it?"

She remembered the effusive manner in which the

Courtiers at the Palace and the King himself had spoken of the Prince.

Now she suspected that their praise of him had not come from their hearts but it was merely because they wished to assure her that she was doing the right thing in bringing her money into their country.

For the first time since she had realised she was a great heiress Athena was afraid.

Her future had not actually meant anything to her in the past. She had been told the money had been left to her and she was very rich, but her father was a wealthy man and she had never wanted for anything since she had been a child.

She had accepted her wealth as she might have accepted the gift of a necklace or a new horse.

She was pleased, but she had not thought about it continually and it did not seem of any particular consequence.

Now she realised how important it was — a passport to marriage. A marriage in which she had no choice and which, even more frightening, the bridegroom had no choice either.

It was an arrangement — a *mariage de convenance* the French called it — and every instinct in Athena fought against the idea.

Now the Prince suddenly assumed frightening proportions.

A man — a man who could make demands upon her because she bore his name, a man who would use her fortune, which would become his on marriage, a man who had no other interest in her as a person.

"I have been ... crazy!" Athena said into the darkness. "How could I have accepted anything so horrible without considering it?"

She put her head back and looked up at the stars. They seemed immeasurably far away and she felt very small and insignificant.

"What does it matter what happens to you?" she felt as if someone asked mockingly.

Then she replied fiercely:

"It *does* matter! I am I. I will not be over-ruled and humiliated in this fashion. I must escape."

The words seemed to come to her almost as if it was a light in the darkness.

Escape! But how? Where could she go? What could she do?

She stared out at the sea, feeling that there must be an answer in the gentle movement of the waves.

Almost mockingly the idea came to her that if she had been a Greek in the old days she would have consulted the Oracle.

The Oracle of Delphi, as her grandmother had always explained to her, had guided and inspired those who consulted it for nine hundred years.

The Greeks had believed that Apollo spoke through the lips of the Pythia. She sat in a cave near the great Temple of Apollo and was a pure young girl trained in priesthood and in the worship of the god.

The Dowager Marchioness had explained to Athena so often what occurred.

"On the day of the Oracle the Pythia bathed in the waters of Castalia and drank from the holy spring. She put on the special robes of prophecy and was led to the Temple of Apollo."

"What happened then, Grandmama?"

"She passed through the main halls of worship until she reached the adyton, the most sacred part of all, the living place of the god where only the priests were allowed to enter."

"Was she afraid?"

"No, dearest, she was dedicated to her work. She took her place on Apollo's throne and she may have taken a branch of the holy laurel in her hand or perhaps she fumigated herself with burnt laurel leaves."

"I knew the laurel was sacred to Apollo," Athena remarked, "but I do not think the leaves could have smelt very nice."

The Dowager Marchioness ignored her.

"Music was played," she went on, her eyes half-closed as if she herself remembered it happening, "and incense was burned."

"And then . . . ?" Athena prompted.

"Then the Pythia fell into a trance and when she was possessed by the god she uttered strange and often wild words that were carefully taken down and later a priest put them into verse."

The Dowager Marchioness went on to tell many stories of what the Pythia had said and how her prophecies had come true.

Athena had sat wide-eyed, listening, believing and almost seeing the pictures her grandmother conjured up.

"If the Oracle was there to-day," she said to herself, "I could go to Delphi and ask Apollo to help and guide me."

Suddenly she was very still.

She knew how near Delphi was to the Summer Palace.

Just around the corner, so to speak, of the promontory projecting into the Gulf of Corinth there was the Krisaean Gulf at the head of which lay the Port of Itea.

This Athena knew, was where the pilgrims, who nearly all went by sea, used to disembark when visiting Delphi. It was in fact at Itea that Lord Byron had landed when he had visited Delphi over thirty years ago.

Athena remembered reading how he and his friend John Hobhouse had been rowed in a strong Cephaloniot ten-oared boat.

Winding in and out of the rocky bays that lined the Gulf they saw a mass of anchored merchant vessels swaying in the moonlight and finally at midnight reached the Port of Itea.

"It is not far away," Athena whispered to herself. "I could go there."

She moved from the balcony into her bed-room and sat down on the bed.

Now a plan was beginning to fall into place almost as if it was a puzzle which she was solving piece by piece.

She had mentioned Delphi to Colonel Stefanatis, but he had not seemed interested.

She had imagined before she left England that all the Greeks, like her grandmother, would be obsessed by their glorious past and by the wonders which still lay only half discovered in their country.

But she learnt from the Greek passengers on board the steamer that they were far too concerned with modern politics to worry much about the past, or else, Athena thought humbly, they had not been interested in talking about their national heritage to her.

But Delphi had shone in her heart like a lighted candle, and she knew that one of the first things she planned to do in Greece was to follow the Sacred Way to the Shrine of Apollo.

Now she knew it would be far easier not to take the long laborious road across the arid foot hills of Parnassus which thousands of pilgrims had trod wearily in the past. Instead she could do what Lord Byron had done and approach Delphi from the sea.

For the first time in her life Athena felt a desire to be independent, to do what she wished without asking approval, without everything being planned for her.

It was almost as if the spirit of Greece that she had felt so strongly like a shining light had entered into her and awoken her to new possibilities within herself.

She felt a wild springing within her mind which had never been there before, a desire to enquire, to find, to know on her own – without being dictated to, without being told what to do.

She was certain as if the Oracle had already spoken, that she must first find her way to Delphi.

She had a guide-book which she had bought in Athens

and it had a rough map of Greece in the front of it.

It was badly printed and badly written, and yet it showed her clearly what a little way she had to travel from where she was now to Port Itea.

That was all that concerned her at the moment, and she knew that once Itea was reached, Lord Byron had climbed towards Delphi which stood above it, built on the cliffs of the mountains where they overlooked the valley of the River Pleistos.

"I will go there, and nothing will stop me," Athena told herself.

As if she could not keep still she walked about her bedroom, thinking out ways and means.

Of one thing she was quite certain – if she asked in the Palace for any help, they would try to stop her.

She would be put off with the usual excuses: nothing could be arranged until the Prince returned – doubtless His Highness had his own plans for taking her to Delphi, just as he would wish to show her other parts of the country!

But how could anyone know that was what he intended?

Doubtless he was as uninterested in the "Ruins" as everybody else appeared to be.

She had been so sure when she left England that, if nothing else, they would have one taste in common which was all-important, the love of Ancient Greece.

A reverence for its teaching, the belief that the whole world owed to the Greeks the beginning of Science and the beginning of philosophical thought.

This was what her grandmother had taught Athena and she had been convinced that the Prince would be still fighting to restore to the world the splendour of the miraculous fifty years when Athens became the centre of civilisation and Apollo and Athena became the gods of Greece.

Now everything she had anticipated was lying in ruins at her feet.

Of course the Prince would not think like that! Why should he? He would be like the other men at the Court of

King Otho who laughed and gossiped and argued about politics.

No-one had offered to take Athena to see the Acropolis, and when she suggested it they had pushed the idea aside as if it was too commonplace and uninteresting to be given a second thought.

She had been too shy to insist, and she had told herself that perhaps the Prince would want to take her there himself.

Then they could dream amongst the marble pillars of the glory of the years when the Acropolis in all its brilliance glowed with light and it served both as a fortress and the sacred sanctuary of Athena.

Athena had imagined that the Prince would explain to her how the Parthenon had looked drenched with colour, blue, scarlet and gold, and containing treasures from all over the Greek world.

They would have walked together, she had thought, to the Erechtheion – the most mysterious and sacred place on the whole Acropolis. Here was the golden lamp that was never allowed to go out, the olive tree Athena had called forth from the ground and the fountain which had sprung up when Poseidon had struck the earth with his trident.

She had imagined herself listening to the stories he would tell her in a deep voice unlike her grandmother's and she had felt herself thrill because she would not be only reliving the story of Greece but would also be with a Greek who loved it as she did.

"Those were just childish dreams," she told herself bitterly. "How could I have been so naïve – so utterly absurd to imagine he would wish to do anything of the sort?"

"I will go home," she decided. "When I meet the Prince I will be strong enough to tell him that I have made a mistake. We have both made one. Perhaps I can give him some of my money in compensation – but I cannot marry him!"

She paused to add:

"I *will* not marry him!"

Then she felt herself tremble because she knew how difficult it would be to make not only the Prince but also her Aunt realise she was serious.

It would seem inconceivable to both of them that at the last moment after coming all this way she should decide not to be a sacrifice to the Prince's need for money.

"Even if he is pleasant and nice to me at the beginning," she told herself, "he will soon want to return to Madame Helena."

The whole impact of what she was thinking and saying to herself swept over her almost like a tidal wave in which she must drown because she had not the strength to swim against it.

Then she told herself that she would survive; but first she must have the strength to refuse to do what everyone wanted, however hard they might try to over-rule her.

It was not going to be easy, Athena was well aware of that.

Her father was a very domineering man and she had always done as he wished ever since her childhood.

Her mother had died when she was ten, and although she remembered her tenderly she had never been an important influence in her life.

It was her grandmother to whom she had turned for affection, for understanding and for guidance.

And now she saw that her grandmother had been concerned less with her than with the Parnassus family.

In arranging this marriage Athena knew she had not thought of her granddaughter's feelings, but of the benefit her money would bring to the reigning Prince of the House of Parnassus.

"How could I have been so stupid, so foolish as not to understand what was happening before I left England?"

Athena knew that if she had been firm and had appealed to her father, who had never been particularly interested in her grandmother's enthusiasm for her native land, she could have prevailed upon him not to agree to her leaving home.

But it was too late to think of that now.

What she had to do now was to extract herself one way or another from the trap into which she had fallen all too willingly, and too easily.

It was a trap – there was no other word for it – and her grandmother had baited it with the glory that had once been Greece, but was certainly not to be found in the Court of their Bavarian King, King Otho.

"I hate them all! I hate them!" Athena cried.

She felt as if they were all intriguing against her, encompassing her about with ropes of silk, which would incarcerate her in Greece with a man who was interested in another woman.

"And why not?" Athena enquired.

She did not blame the Prince.

Of course there were other women in his life. Doubtless there were women he wished to marry but could not afford to do so.

But being married to a rich Englishwoman would not prevent him from loving where he wished and doing what he wanted.

There would be nothing left for her but a cage of pomp and circumstance and a title in which she was not in the least interested.

"What shall I do?"

The question came again and she knew the answer.

She would go to Delphi and if she could not consult the Oracle at least she felt that somehow she would be near the gods who had once reigned in Greece – the gods whose Empire had not been over great tracts of land or a subject people.

In the person of Apollo the Greeks had conquered the world by the power of beauty.

He had no earthly resources, no Army, no Navy, no powerful Government, but he had captured men's minds, and in the silence Athena was still certain she would hear the voice of the god calling to her own heart to seek the light.

"I will go to Delphi."

Nothing, she told herself, was impossible!

At Delphi she would know what to do and she would no longer be afraid.

She caught a glimpse of herself in the mirror as she moved across the bed-room and it seemed to her that in the past hour she had grown from a very young English girl into a woman.

She did not know how it had happened – she only knew that, as she had always known they would, the gods had helped her and were showing her the way.

Chapter Two

The caique with the wind in its sails rounded the tip of the promontory and Athena gave a sigh that was one both of relief and joy.

She had done it! She had escaped!

Even now she could hardly believe she was free of the Palace and the ship now out of sight of anyone who might be looking out at such an early hour.

She had made her plans very carefully and it had given her an excitement she had never known to arrange matters for herself. She had tried to think of every detail, not only of her requirements, but also of eventualities that might betray her at the last moment.

She had of course been unable to sleep, but she had lain on her bed after packing in the Greek bag which had been woven by native craftsmen the few necessities she thought she might need.

She had written a letter to her Aunt in which she had said that as she was tired of waiting for the Prince she had decided to stay for a night or perhaps two with friends who lived nearby.

She begged her Aunt not to worry and said that she would be perfectly safe and they would look after her.

She smiled as she wrote the pronoun, thinking her Aunt would not appreciate the fact that *"they"* as far as she was concerned were the gods who dwelt at Delphi.

She had drawn back the curtains from her window and from her bed she could watch the sky. Long before dawn, when she saw the stars beginning to fade, she had risen to dress herself.

This was quite a feat as she was used to having a maid or even two in attendance.

She had chosen her gown very carefully the night before. All those in her trousseau were elaborate, their full skirts decorated with lace and frills.

But one was comparatively simple with a plain skirt and for the tiny waist a blue sash which a child might have worn.

Athena chose her plainest bonnet to go with it, and thinking it might be cool in the ship she carried over her arm a warm shawl.

When she was dressed she knew the most difficult part of the whole adventure was to get out of the Palace without being seen.

But she had listened during the night to the movements of the night-watchmen walking around inside and the footsteps of the sentries pacing outside.

Methodically she had calculated the exact time when she could get down the stairs without being noticed and when she could cross the garden to reach the sanctuary of the bushes before the sentry turned and marched back in the direction from which he had come.

The actual exit from the Palace was easy, because she had found a door into the garden the previous day which she noted without realising it at the time was easy to open from the inside.

The top half of the door was of glass and she had thought that it seemed a vulnerable place to leave unguarded when the great door of the Palace itself had sentries on either side of it.

As she sped across the grass into the shade of the hibiscus bushes she thought that if a sentry saw her in her white gown he would think she was a ghost or some sprite from the underworld bemusing his senses and would not challenge her.

But actually the sentry was looking in the opposite direction and Athena climbed over the low wall which separated the Palace from the road which ran along the cliffs, and stood looking down at the sea beneath her.

The Palace had been built high up on the mountainside and the Harbour of Mikis at which she had arrived was on the west coast of the Gulf while beyond it was a small town of the same name.

She had realised when she arrived that from the harbour to the Palace on the twisting, turning road which made the climb easy for the horses was at least two miles.

But by going straight downhill Athena reckoned that the harbour in actual fact was not more than a quarter of that distance away.

It proved to be a little further than she had anticipated, but Athena was a country girl and used to walking and riding long distances. She reached the Harbour of Mikis without being unduly fatigued and in surprisingly quick time.

Now the sky had lightened perceptibly and all around was the translucent grey of the prelude to the rising of the sun.

It would have been impossible, Athena thought, to imagine there could be so many shades of that mysterious, elusive colour, ranging from the silver grey of the sea and the pigeon-feathered grey of the cliffs on the other side of the water, to the deep almost purple-grey of the mountains.

There was however, no time for day-dreaming or even for admiring the view.

She found as she had expected that the fishermen were already astir, carrying their yellow nets aboard their caiques, shouting cheerily to each other or singing a song as they got their boats ready for the sea.

She found an elderly man who seemed less busy than the others and told him what she required.

She spoke slowly in her perfect Greek and he understood her without any difficulty.

"A ship to take you to Itea, lady?" he asked scratching his head. "They'll all be going fishing."

"I will make it worth their while," Athena promised. "I will pay for the journey there and for the return. It will doubtless come to more than they would earn by a day's fishing."

It took a little time and quite an amount of argument before the elderly man persuaded the crew of one of the caiques to accept the large sum of money which Athena offered in return for their services.

Finally with a great many smiles and good-humoured chaffing they agreed to abandon their nets and the caique set off.

The dawn wind billowed out its sails, and when the twelve men dipped their oars into the waves the water fell from them like glittering diamonds.

As they moved Athena kept looking apprehensively over her shoulder at the Palace high above them.

She was quite certain that no-one would be watching the Harbour at this hour of the morning, and yet at the same time she was thankful now finally they were out of sight and round into the Gulf of Krisa.

Now the mountains rose high on each side of the gulf and as the first rays of the sun came up over the horizon their tops were turned to gold and every other colour of the rainbow filtered across them.

It was so lovely that Athena felt as if the time she was at sea sped past and she could hardly believe they had been travelling for some hours when at last they reached the Port of Itea.

There were several anchored merchant vessels with their three high sail-less masts swaying on the waves, but there was not the galaxy of them that Lord Byron had seen.

She found on arrival as she stepped out of the boat that there were a few gaily decorated horses and donkeys waiting to carry anyone who engaged them up the long steep climb to Delphi.

Athena, who had a good knowledge of horse-flesh, refused the donkeys which were pressed on her by their owners, and chose instead a young horse which she felt would carry her more swiftly.

She also liked the honest, good-humoured face of its owner.

All the animals soliciting the tourists had thick saddles made of sacking covered with a woollen rug on which the rider could sit sideways in comparative comfort.

It meant that no horsemanship was required because the owner of the animal led it up the hill, and Athena had a sudden longing to ride on her own without restrictions as she had once imagined she might ride with the Prince over his land.

But she was aware that the owner of the young horse was obviously both fond and proud of his possession and would not let the bridle out of his hands.

She was therefore prepared to be carried without any effort up the winding stony path which was so steep that she felt at times it was almost cruel to make her horse carry any weight on its back even someone as light as herself.

The countryside was extraordinarily beautiful and Athena kept turning her head from side to side, afraid she might miss some exquisite piece of scenery simply because she was looking the other way.

At the bottom of the valley there was the River Pleistos and on either side of it rolled grove upon grove of silvery olive trees, their ancient trunks and twisting branches seeming to Athena to be redolent with history.

They passed caves which she longed to explore and she remembered that Lord Byron had almost been lost in one.

But her goal was Delphi and she did not dare to linger on the way.

High above her she was vividly conscious of the great Shining Cliffs, the Phaedriades, which scintillated in the sunlight with a myriad points of multi-coloured reflected light.

She remembered how her grandmother had told her that

when Apollo left the holy island of Delos to conquer Greece a dolphin had guided his ship through the Krisaean Gulf which lay beneath the Shining Cliffs.

"The young god," the Dowager Marchioness had said, "leapt from the sea disguised as a star at high noon. Flames soared from him and the flash of splendour lit the sky."

She paused dramatically, then she said softly:

"Then the star vanished and there was only a handsome young man armed with a bow and arrows."

Athena had listened breathlessly.

"He marched up the steep road to the lair of the dragon," the Dowager Marchioness went on, "and when it was slain he announced in a clear ringing voice to the gods that he claimed possession of all the territory he could see from where he was standing."

"It was a lovely place," Athena had murmured.

"Apollo was amongst other things the god of good taste and he had chosen the most haunting and satisfying view in Greece," the Dowager Marchioness replied.

Half way up the steep ascent Athena looked back and knew that her grandmother had not exaggerated.

There was the blue sea in the distance, the valley of silver-grey olive trees below, the blue mountains curving away to the left and the right and the River Pleistos like a silver ribbon running through the centre of the valley.

She turned her head to look up. The Shining Cliffs rose ahead, grey and silver, they seemed to glitter in the sunshine and she had the feeling that the valley, the mountains and the sea were slowly revolving in front of them.

The man leading her horse brought her back to reality by telling her that there used to be wolves in the caves they had just passed but they had not been seen for some years.

Athena was not afraid of the wolves; what excited her far more than wild animals were the flowers.

Never had she imagined the grassland up which they were climbing could be so vivid with colour.

She recognised grape hyacinths, the star of Bethlehem, narcissus, anemones, poppies and of course the redolent thyme. There were also wild orchids and vividly blue blossoms to which she could not put a name besides the wild iris, the flower of the gods.

Higher and higher they climbed, even the young horse finding it hard going, until finally they had reached the narrow dusty road which had been the Sacred Way and stood below the Shining Cliffs themselves.

Above her through the blossoming fruit trees Athena could see several broken pillars and the outline of what appeared to be a Temple and she knew that she had reached her goal.

It all lay to the right of a small, untidy village, many of the houses built precariously on the very edge of the cliff, the others lying haphazard amongst the ruins, children were sitting astride a great marble block and making mud-pies on the flat surface of another.

Athena dismounted, paid the man so generously that he was almost over-profuse in his thanks, then stood staring up at the cliffs above her.

She saw wheeling high against the sky a bird that she was sure was an eagle and remembered that Lord Byron had seen a flight of twelve which he had taken as a sign that Apollo and the Muses had accepted his offering of "Childe Harold".

Athena was certain that the eagle was a good omen for her too, and now because she was impatient to see what had brought her here she started to climb up the hillside.

She found steps amongst the grasses and occasionally exquisite pieces of carving that she felt should be taken away to safety rather than left uncared for and unattended.

She had known that little was left of the great Temple of Apollo except a few broken columns. But she was not primarily looking for remnants of the antiquities: she was really seeking to feel and understand what this sacred place had meant to the Ancient Greeks.

When she was a little higher up the mountainside the

white stone gleamed like fire and she had a feeling of quietness and serenity and that the Shining Cliffs protected something very precious and sacred.

Avoiding the village she climbed higher and higher still, finding the walking hard until finally she found what she knew must be the Stadium.

There were only what must have been the upper row of seats above the ground and the rest was overgrown with grasses and moss.

Athena tried to imagine the competitors with their perfect, athletic bodies competing amongst themselves.

She sat down to get her breath and recited the ode written by Pindar in praise of the Aeginetan Aristomenes, who had won a wrestling match here at Delphi in 446 B.C.

> "He who has won some new splendour
>   Rides on the air
>   Borne upwards on the wings of his human vigour
>   In the fierce pride of hope, rejoicing
>   In no desire for wealth, enjoying
>   For a brief space the exaltation of glory."

All the Athletes competed naked, their slim, muscular bodies as perfect as those of the gods they worshipped.

Athena sat for a long time in the Stadium. Then slowly she began the descent back to the Temple of Apollo, then lower still, seeking to the left of it the ravine where the Oracle had been.

It was, however, difficult for her to know the exact spot where the prophecies had taken place.

Then because she remembered that her grandmother had spoken of the Temple of Athena below the Sacred Way, she crossed the road and found hidden among the olive trees three perfect columns on a circular foundation which she knew had been dedicated to Athena.

They seemed to have a special light about them and the grasses which grew round the stones which had fallen from the Temple seemed to contain brighter and more brilliant flowers than any she had seen before.

Athena stared at them for a long time, and then because she was conscious that her legs were aching from the stiff climb up to the Stadium she sat down amongst the grasses and rested her back against a block of white marble.

She felt as if the faith of all those who had worshipped here so many centuries ago was still vibrant and alive, and she felt the prayers of those who had brought the Goddess Athena their petitions still lingered on the warm air.

A movement in the sky attracted her attention. Athena lifted her head and looked up.

There were eagles just as she imagined they would be hovering over the Shrine. There were six of them and the great span of their wings made them seem omnipotent – King of Birds – surveying in awful majesty the weakness of the mortals beneath them.

Silhouetted against the sun they seemed to shine with a light of their own and she watched them fascinated, until it seemed to her as if she herself was amongst them soaring in the sky, moving always higher and higher towards the sun...

* * *

How long she slept Athena had no idea but she came slowly back to mortal consciousness to realise that she was not alone. Someone was with her.

For a moment it was only a shadowy thought and she was still with the eagles.

Half-asleep, hardly conscious of what she was doing or saying Athena murmured:

"I was ... flying into the ... sun."

The sound of her own voice made her open her eyes.

Sitting looking at her as she lay amongst the flowers was a man. For a moment she looked at him hazily, finding it hard to focus her sight.

"I was certain you were a goddess," he said in an amused voice, "but I am not sure if you are Aphrodite or Athena herself."

Without thinking, without considering what she was saying, Athena answered him.

"My name is Athena," she said, and woke up completely.

"Then I offer you my most respectful homage," he said a little mockingly.

Athena sat up and put her hands to her hair. She had taken off her bonnet as she had climbed down the twisting path from the Stadium because it had been so hot.

Now she realised that she must look very strange lying bareheaded amongst the flowers and what was more, talking to a strange man to whom she had not been introduced.

He was certainly very unlike the men she had met at home, and yet despite his appearance she was sure he was well-bred.

He was wearing a white shirt without a tie and with the sleeves rolled up above the elbows of his sun-burnt arms. But when she looked at his face Athena forgot everything else.

He had in fact the perfect classical features she had expected to find on every Greek, only at the Court of King Otho, at any rate, to be disappointed.

As she stared at him he smiled at her and the smile took away the almost severe perfection of his face and made him very human.

His deep set eyes were twinkling and she thought to herself that they had the light of Apollo in them.

"We have now established that you are the goddess Athena," the strange man said, still speaking in English. "Perhaps I should introduce myself or would you prefer to guess my identity?"

His tone made Athena feel self-conscious and the colour rose in her cheeks as she said a little uncomfortably:

"I ... I am sorry ... I was asleep when you spoke to me ... and I did not know what I was ... saying."

"You told me you were flying into the sun," the man said, "and surely no human being – if you are human – could ask for more."

Athena made a movement as if she would rise.

"I think... I should be... going."

"Going where?" the man asked. "Unless you are returning to Olympus from whence you must have come."

She smiled at him because she could not help it.

"You are very... flattering," she said. "But I feel this is a very strange conversation to have with... someone I have never met... before."

"We have met now," he said firmly, "and you have not answered my question."

As if it was a game in which she must take part, Athena said:

"You are not Apollo – you are too dark."

"I assure you I would not presume to such an exalted position as that of the god of light," her companion said, "even though I am a pale reflection of him. Try again."

Athena thought for a moment, then she said:

"Then you are not Hermes. I was thinking of him as I came up the hill from the Port, feeling he would protect me because after all he is the god of travellers as well as the messenger of the gods."

"If that is who you wish me to be, then I am quite content to become Hermes," the man answered, "but actually my name is Orion."

"The most famous and the most beautiful of all the constellations of stars!" Athena exclaimed.

"Now I am indeed flattered. Is your name really Athena?"

She nodded her head.

"Yes, really."

"And yet you are English?"

"Is it so obvious?"

"Only because you speak English. Otherwise you might be pure Greek, Athena when very young – not yet old enough to be the goddess of wisdom, but old enough to be the goddess of love."

Again Athena blushed, and now she picked her bonnet up from where she had laid it beside her.

"Do not put it on," Orion said quickly. "Your hair is perfect. Just the right colour against the marble and your eyes are the grey of the sea in the early morning."

Instinctively Athena's face turned towards the Gulf of Krisa as it could be glimpsed through the rocks beyond the carpet of olive trees.

"Also your nose is pure Greek," Orion finished.

"That is what I have been told before," Athena replied, "and it makes me very ... proud."

"You would like to be Greek?"

"I have a little Greek blood in my veins and perhaps that has made me want all my life to be here, as I am now."

There was a little throb in her voice which told the man listening how much it moved her.

"And you came here alone?" he asked in surprise.

He looked beyond her through the trees as if he thought somebody else might be slumbering there whom he had not yet perceived.

"Quite alone," Athena answered.

Then she wondered if she had been indiscreet in telling him so much about herself.

"That was brave of you," he said. "English ladies are seldom so adventurous. They come here in a party, and if the majesty of Apollo makes them feel awe-inspired they giggle with each other because they are embarrassed to admit the emotions he arouses in them."

"You are speaking very scathingly," Athena said. "Do you not like the English?"

"Not very much," he admitted. "Not the ones I have met so far."

"Then it is certainly time for me to leave."

"You know I did not mean that," he said in his deep voice.

Now he looked into her eyes.

"You are different – different from the average Englishwoman. But everyone who comes to Delphi is a pilgrim and as such acceptable to the gods, wherever they may have been born."

"How I wish I could have seen this place in all its glory," Athena sighed.

"There have been many Temples in this particular place," Orion said quietly. "The first was a very small shrine made of bees-wax and feathers. The second was of ferns twisted together."

He paused.

"The third of laurel-boughs; the fourth of bronze with golden song-birds perched on the roof."

"I would like to have seen that one," Athena interposed softly.

"The fifth was of stone," he went on, "which was burnt down in 489 B.C., the sixth was destroyed by an earthquake, finally about 400 A.D., the seventh was plundered and torn down by the Christian Emperor Arçadius."

He hesitated for a moment before he continued:

"But long before that the Emperor Nero had robbed the Sacred Shrine of seven hundred bronze statues and removed them to Rome."

There was a note in his voice which told Athena how he resented the manner in which the Romans had appropriated treasures that were Greek. Then thinking of the Elgin Marbles she was silent.

"So much has been taken from us," Orion went on, "but they cannot take away the feeling that Apollo is still here."

"No shelter has Apollo, nor sacred laurel leaves;
The fountains now are silent; the voice is stilled."

Athena spoke in a low voice and he turned to look at her in surprise.

"Is that what you feel?"

"No," she answered, "that is what the Oracle said to the Emperor Julian the Apostate when he came here in A.D. 362 and asked what he could do to preserve the glory of the god."

"How do you know all these things?" Orion enquired. "Who has taught you?"

"I have heard the stories of Greek mythology ever since I was a child," Athena answered. "That is why I have always longed to come here and why, even though I see how little there is left to see, I am not disappointed."

She felt that his eyes lit up at her words.

"You belong here," he said quietly, and she knew that he could not have paid her a greater compliment.

They sat talking for a long time.

Orion who obviously knew everything that was known about Delphi, told to her more details of the Oracle than her grandmother had told her and described many of the ceremonies which had taken place when the pilgrims landed in the Port below and flooded along the Sacred Way.

Apollo had ordered them to come in high summer and the scorching sunlight flashed off the rocks and the white and gold glory of his Temple must have shimmered almost blindingly.

"They came very slowly," Orion said, "and yet there were always those who wished to lay their heart and their soul at the feet of Apollo. On one single day 50,000 pilgrims crowded through the Port of Itea."

He paused, then he said:

"To-day there is hardly a visitor and after all what is there for them to see?"

"Perhaps like us," Athena said, "they come to feel the presence of Apollo, and perhaps to hear within themselves the voice of the Oracle."

Orion looked at her in surprise.

"Is that why you are here?"

She did not wish to tell him the truth, but she felt as if he forced it from between her lips.

"Yes."

"The Oracle has gone," he said, "but I think that not the Pythia but Athena will speak to you. How could she fail to listen to her namesake?"

"Perhaps no-one can solve our problems except ourselves," Athena said.

She wondered as she spoke how she could be talking to a man she had never met before in this intimate manner.

Yet because he was a stranger, because he had appeared from nowhere while she was asleep, and because he could be of no importance in her life, it seemed easy and natural.

With anyone from her own world she would have felt constrained. Besides never had she been able to talk to any man of her thoughts and feelings or of the gods and goddesses that to her were so real.

Always the conversation must be of sport or of general affairs; but this man, whoever he might be, was different.

It was obvious that to him Apollo and Athena were as real as they were to her, and so she was able to say what came into her mind and after the first few moments of waking not to feel embarrassed.

The olive trees sheltered them from a sun that was scorchingly hot in the first part of the afternoon, then gradually the air grew a little cooler and finally almost regretfully, because she could not bear the thought that their conversation must come to an end Athena said tentatively:

"Perhaps you could tell me of a place where I could find something to eat and stay the night?"

"You intend to stay here?" Orion asked.

Athena looked down into the valley.

It would take her at least two hours, she thought, to reach the Port of Itea.

It would be getting late when she arrived there and she was certain that it would be difficult to persuade the fishermen to venture out into the dark on the voyage round to Mikis.

It would be better to leave early in the morning. She would be back at noon and perhaps, she thought, then she would feel stronger to face her Aunt's anger at the manner in which she had disappeared.

Somehow she could not bear this perfect day to be disrupted by disagreeableness as must inevitably occur if she arrived back at the Palace very late to-night.

Orion appeared to be waiting for her answer and after a moment she said:

"I would like to stay here if it is possible. I feel too tired to go all the way back to Itea, even if the horse on which I came here has waited to convey me down again."

"It has doubtless waited," Orion said with a smile, "as his owner knows that you will require his services. At the same time I think you are wise to stay the night. There is only one Taverna I can recommend. It is on the other side of the village and it is primitive. But it is clean and you will be welcome."

"Would you be so kind as to show me the way there?" Athena asked.

There did not seem to her to be anything reprehensible in asking this stranger for guidance. Somehow she had the feeling that he would protect her.

Perhaps because she had been so cosseted and looked after all her life it had made her more trusting than another woman might have been.

At the same time because of what they had said to each other and the manner in which they had talked together she felt a confidence in him that she had never felt for any other man.

"If you have had nothing to eat all day you must be very hungry," he said. "I should have thought of it before, but we were feeding our minds rather than our bodies."

That was what Athena thought and she flashed him a smile as she rose to her feet.

He picked up the bag in which she had put her few requirements and she remembered how heavy it had seemed when she had to carry it all the way up to the Stadium.

She did not attempt to put on her bonnet, not only because Orion had asked her not to but also because it gave her a feeling of freedom and lightness to be without it.

She was well aware that her Aunt and all her other relations would think it very reprehensible for a lady to be walking about without a covering on her head and especially to be accompanied by a man in his shirt sleeves with his collar open.

Then Athena told herself they would never understand why she was here or what it had meant to her to come to Delphi.

She admitted that her delight had been not only in the Sacred Shrine but also in having someone who understood, to talk to about it. Someone who she felt now was in fact protecting her and looking after her as the god Hermes might have done.

They moved through the olive trees, then climbed some rough steps onto the road above.

For a moment they both stood looking up at the Shining Cliffs and at the great ravine on one side of it from which a cascade of water fell silver and shimmering onto the rocks below.

"Is that the water of Castalia which Byron found to have a 'villainous tang'?" Athena asked.

"It may have been," Orion replied, "but I think you need something more sustaining than water, however blessed. So I suggest we seek the Taverna where they have quite a passable local wine and delicious coffee."

"You are making me feel thirsty, and I admit to feeling very hungry," Athena said. "It is rather lowering to realise that while our minds and hearts are in the heights our bodies are still mundane enough to remain very material."

"I shall never believe that of your body," Orion replied. "As I suspected when I saw you this afternoon, you move like a goddess with a grace that only the nymphs that sprang from the spray of the waves could emulate."

Athena gave a little laugh.

"I like your compliments," she said. "They are so different from any I have ever received before."

"And you have obviously received very many," he said mockingly.

"Not really," she answered.

Now there was a wistful note in her voice as she remembered that the compliments she had received in Athens and which at first had seemed so delightful had doubtless been lip-service to her fortune rather than to herself.

It struck her as they moved along through the village that was built above and below the Sacred Way that this was the first time in her life that anyone was talking to her without being aware of her background or her rank as her father's daughter.

To this strange man, Orion, she was just Athena. He accepted that as her name and asked no further questions.

Yet they had conversed as equals in the manner of two scholars who had met each other across the centuries of time and to whom there was nothing of importance except the searchings of each other's minds.

"While I commend your courage," Orion was saying as they walked along, "at the same time I do not advise you to make many such expeditions in Greece without being accompanied either by someone older than yourself or at least a courier."

"Why not?" Athena enquired.

"The first reason is obvious," he replied. "You are young and you are very beautiful."

"And another?"

"There are always bandits in this part of the world."

"Bandits?" Athena exclaimed.

"Bandits – brigands – whatever you like to call them," he replied. "They have no respect for property nor in some cases for the female sex."

Athena remembered that when she was in Athens she had soon found that the most talked about person at Court was an Albanian General.

She had been told with bated breath that he was a Pallikare who was certainly amongst the most striking of the many races who were crowded into the city.

"They are a legendary lot," someone had said in her presence, "mercenaries and cut-throats, and originally bandits from the Albanian mountains."

"It is all very well to disparage them," another man answered, "but they fought magnificently in the War of Independence and it is to keep them amiably disposed that the King has named their Chief, General Xristodolous Hadji-Petros as one of his *aides-de-camp*."

The General was certainly a splendid figure, Athena thought.

Ferocious-looking, he wore an Albanian costume with crimson and gold embroideries and he bristled with pistols and *yetaghans*.

His horses' bridles and saddles were decorated with gold and silver and his men, with long moustachios, swaggered about in great shaggy cloaks and looked like bears.

It was during the week that Athena had spent in Athens that a sensational scandal had broken.

A famous English beauty, Lady Ellenborough, who after a very chequered career in which, it was whispered, she had been not only King Otho's mistress but also previously that of his father, King Ludwig of Bavaria, had run away with the General into the mountains.

Despite his magnificent appearance he was over sixty, a widower with children.

But among those who had been very conscious of his attractions was Queen Amelia, and apparently she, as Athena heard, was furious and jealous that the General should have eloped with someone who moved in Court circles.

No-one, Athena remembered, had talked of anything else and she suspected that one of the reasons that her Aunt had been so insistent on leaving Athens for the Prince's Palace at Mikis was to prevent her hearing more about the scandal that had left everyone gasping at its audacious impropriety.

But at Delphi, amongst the untidy houses which were little more than huts or hovels, she could not imagine she would find a brigand looking like the Albanian General.

As if he read her thoughts Orion said:

"There are brigands and brigands, some are extremely picturesque, but others can be dangerous and that is why I am warning you against them, Athena."

"I am not inviting their company," Athena laughed.

He stopped still and looked at her and because he had ceased walking she was forced to do the same.

"Look at me," he said.

Wondering she turned her eyes up to his.

He was so much taller than her that his head seemed to be silhouetted against the sky.

"You must take care of yourself," he said very quietly but insistently. "You are so beautiful – so unbelievably beautiful – and I realise so innocent, that you have no idea of the dangers that might be waiting for you. Promise me, promise me by everything you hold sacred that you will be careful."

The solemnity in his voice gave her a very strange feeling.

No-one had ever spoken to her like that before, no-one's voice had ever suggested so much concern – and another emotion to which she could not put a name.

"I will ... be careful."

"You promise?"

"I promise!"

It was an easy promise to make, she thought, for after to-morrow she was quite certain there would never be another chance to escape.

They would be watching for her, and if she was brave enough, as she intended, to tell the Prince she could not marry him, she would go back to the safety of England where there were no brigands, but also no gods or sacred shrines.

They walked on and now as if Orion was thinking deeply he did not speak.

When they left a larger part of the village behind, the narrow road began to slope upwards.

Finally they climbed steeply to where on the outskirts

of the other houses there stood what was obviously a Taverna with a breath-taking view over the valley beneath them.

It was a very simple building of two storeys and like all the houses in the village had a flat roof. It had a front porch made simply of dried branches of trees supported by wooden struts.

Beneath it were a number of deal tables at which were sitting several elderly men looking, Athena thought, as if they were customers of long standing.

They said good-evening in a friendly manner to Orion when they both appeared, and he answered them, calling them by their names as if they were his close friends.

Carrying Athena's bag and putting a hand under her elbow as if to support her he drew her through the doorway and into the house itself.

There was a large kitchen, a table in the centre of it and a stove at one side.

A middle-aged woman and a young girl dressed in peasant costume were preparing a meal while a thickset man whose hair was turning grey was sitting in an arm-chair, smoking a pipe.

They looked up as Orion and Athena entered and there was no doubt of the curiosity in their expressions.

"Madame Argeros, I have brought you a lady who requires a bed for the night," Orion said. "I told her that you will welcome her and she will be safe in your comfortable house, safe from the brigands and the 'sharks' in the village who batten upon tourists."

Madame Argeros laughed.

"Any friend of yours, Orion, is welcome," she said. "The lady can have Nonika's room. She can move in with us."

They spoke in Greek but Athena understood.

"I would not wish to be any trouble," she said in their language.

Orion stared at her in astonishment.

"You speak Greek!" he exclaimed. "We have been together all the afternoon and you did not tell me."

"You did not ask me, and you spoke English so well that I might have been put to shame."

"But you speak with perfection!" he said. "Like everything else about you."

The last words were spoken in English so that only she could understand them. Athena felt shy and did not look at him.

"Let me introduce you," Orion said. "Madame Argeros, the best cook in the whole province, Dimitrios Argeros, her husband, the owner of this comfortable Taverna and Nonika, the prettiest girl for miles around."

Nonika blushed and dropped her eyes, Dimitrios Argeros gave Athena a respectful nod, but he did not rise from the chair on which he was sitting.

"Come and sit down," Madame Argeros suggested. "Nonika will get your room ready."

"We are both thirsty and hungry, Madame," Orion said. "I have not eaten since breakfast and I have not asked my friend when she last enjoyed a meal."

"As it happens it was last night," Athena replied, "with the exception of an orange which one of the boatmen gave me on my way here."

She spoke in Greek and Madame Argeros gave a little cry of horror.

"You must be starving!" she said. "Sit down, child, and I will find you something to eat, but dinner is not yet ready."

Obediently Athena sat down at the large deal table and Madame put down in front of her a loaf of bread and a cheese made from sheep's milk which Athena had tasted before and found delicious.

There were black olives ripe from the sun and red tomatoes sliced into their own juice, besides a cucumber hastily cut and added to the plate of tomatoes.

The bread was crisp and delicious and without waiting Athena cut herself a slice and spread on it the white sheep's-milk cheese.

As she did so Orion brought a bottle of wine to the table, opened it and poured her out a glass.

She sipped it.

"A feast for the gods," she smiled. "I do not believe that even ambrosia and nectar could taste better when I am so hungry."

He laughed, helped himself to the olives and also cut a large piece of the bread.

"You are not to spoil your appetite, Orion," Madame admonished from the stove. "I have cooked all your favourite dishes as you are leaving us to-morrow."

"Shall I guess?" he asked. "Or shall I tell you I can already smell the fragrance of baby lamb?"

"It is to be a surprise," Madame said severely. "There is *Moussaka* to start and I only hope your friend enjoys it as much as you do."

"She will," Orion answered.

He smiled at Athena as he spoke and as he did so it suddenly struck her that she had never been so happy in the whole of her life.

She was with people who welcomed her because she was herself.

She was with a man who was speaking to her as an intellectual equal.

This was what she had always wanted, what she had always missed. It could be summed up in one word – happiness.

Chapter Three

Nonika came shyly into the kitchen to tell Athena her room was ready.

"I expect you would like Nonika to show you the way upstairs," Orion suggested.

"Thank you, I would," Athena replied.

She picked up the hand-woven bag and her bonnet from where they were laid on a chair and followed Nonika.

They climbed a narrow, rather rickety staircase, and on the low-ceilinged small landing at the top Athena saw there were two doors, one on the right the other on the left.

Nonika opened the one on the left and Athena followed her into a room which contained a bed, a wool rug on the wooden floor and a chest-of-drawers on which there was a small mirror.

Another table contained a washing basin and there was one chair, but nothing else against the white-washed walls. But it was spotlessly clean, and smelt of bees-wax and wild thyme.

"It is very kind of you to give me your room," Athena said.

"I only sleep here when there are no guests," Nonika replied. "Orion has the other room."

"You know him well and he stays here often?" Athena enquired.

She felt perhaps she had no right to ask the question. At the same time she could not help feeling curious about Orion's position in the household.

He was so obviously a different class from the Argeros family, but they appeared to treat him as if he was a favoured son rather than a client of their Taverna.

While they were eating Madame had admonished him for having missed the midday meal, and her husband had cracked jokes and repeated some incident that had happened in the village to people who were apparently known to them both.

In answer to Athena's question Nonika gave a little shrug of her shoulders.

"He comes – he goes," she said enigmatically. "Sometimes we do not see him for a long time, but always he returns and is welcome."

She gave Athena a smile as she added:

"As you are welcome as his friend."

She shut the door as she spoke and Athena felt herself warm at the sincerity of her words.

How charming and simple these people were, she thought, so different from the sharp-eyed, wise-cracking society notabilities whom she had met in Athens.

Even the Parnassus relations who had come to call on her had seemed very social-minded in their outlook and the women were extremely fashionable in their appearance.

She realised that the whole of Athenian society centred around the Court and the gossip that enthralled them left little room for any other interest or amusement.

It was not extraordinary that the Courtiers and notabilities who circled round King Otho and Queen Amelia should have a passion for scandal.

It ran through the Salons and cafés of the whole city and was in keeping with its many other Oriental traits.

Athens had surprised Athena in that it was not in the least what she had expected from the Greek Capital.

"It is part Turkish, part Slav and part Levantine," one of the King's *aides-de-camp* had explained to her, and she realised when she drove through the busy city that he was right.

There were the seething Turkish Bazaars, the cafés where at least half the population spent most of their time smoking their *nargailyes* and drinking innumerable cups of coffee.

But what had delighted Athena was the noisy crowded streets where she could see the exotic costumes which were characteristic of the islands and the provinces.

This was where she longed to wander by herself if she had been allowed, to watch the people and have the opportunity of entering the dark churches, decorated with Icons, from where, as she passed, she could hear the chanting of the monks.

The King's Palace, plain, square and uncompromisingly Bavarian, had set the standard for the taste of Greek Society, who were determined to be as European as possible.

But however conventional they might wish to be, Athens remained a conglomeration of booths and Palaces, noisy *gargottes* and Byzantine churches.

"You would hardly believe it," someone said to Athena: "the city has over twenty thousand inhabitants but only two thousand houses."

"Then where do they all sleep?" Athena asked.

"Many of them in the streets," was the answer.

In the short time she was there Athena realised that the tiny capital attracted like a magnet pleasure seekers from all over the Balkans.

Rich Moldavian nobles travelled for weeks over immense distances to indulge in riotous living; fezes, turbans, and the lambskin hats of the Caucasians intermingled with tasselled caps.

A mixture of yashmaked kohl-eyed women wrapped anonymously in black rubbed shoulders with colourful peasants, and ladies wearing silks and satins direct from Paris.

It was only in the Palace and in its splendid gardens that Athena had felt lonely among the chattering groups of nobles and her eyes went continually toward the Parthenon standing sentinel over the city as it had done for more than two thousand years.

She wanted to say with Byron:

> "Ah! Greece! They love thee least who owe thee most;
> Their birth, their blood and that sublime record
> Of hero sires, who shame thy now degenerate horde!"

But because she was so anxious to love everything in the land in which she was to live and because she wanted to immerse herself in everything that was Greek, she would not admit that Athens had disappointed her or that the Greek people whom she met had not in any way measured up to her expectations.

But to-day she had found in Orion the type of man she had hoped to meet.

This was how she had imagined all Greek men would look and that they would be proud of their past, trying within themselves to revive the spirit which had made Greece the foundation on which European civilization was built.

As she washed, then tidied her hair, Athena could not help wishing that she could change her dress and put on one of the exquisite gowns she had brought with her from London in her trousseau.

But she laughed at the idea of going downstairs to the kitchen bedecked in silk and tulle or wearing one of the off-the-shoulder gowns edged with a lace bertha which was the fashion.

At the same time something very feminine within her wanted Orion to see her at her best.

How could he judge what she was like in the very plain dress she had chosen in which to travel to Delphi?

Then she told herself she was being ridiculous.

"To-morrow he is leaving and I shall never see him again," she told her reflection and wondered why the thought gave her a pain that was almost physical within her breast.

Laughing at her vanity, and yet at the same time driven by it, she arranged her hair more fashionably.

She brushed the ringlets on either side of her face until they shone as if they had caught the sunlight, and made certain that the parting down the centre of her small head was absolutely straight.

The face she saw in the mirror had changed, she felt, in some way from its look before she had come to Delphi.

Her large grey eyes which dominated the oval of her face had a light in them that had not been there before, there was a touch of colour in her cheeks and her lips were soft and parted with excitement.

Only her small straight nose which her grandmother had always said was exactly like that of the goddess after whom she was named, remained the same.

Yet the whole effect was different, though Athena could not explain exactly how.

She remembered when Homer wished to describe the goddess Athena he called her "the bright-eyed one", and that he had spoken of Helen of Troy as "wearing a shining veil".

"That is what is happening to me now," Athena said to herself. "I am shining with a reflection from the Shining Cliffs and from the light that I felt in the Temple."

Because she was in a hurry to go downstairs to see Orion again and talk to him, she did not linger long in her bedroom.

Just for a moment she glanced out through the window at the stupendous view that lay beneath.

Now as the sun was sinking the valley was in deep shadow, the olive trees no longer silver-grey but like a dark carpet of purple.

But the little Port of Itea still glowed in the setting sun and the tops of the mountains were burnished with gold.

Athena drew in her breath. Then spurred by an urgency that she was afraid to explain to herself she hurried below.

There was a cloth on the table in the kitchen and when Orion rose at her entrance she saw that he had put on a black velvet coat over his shirt.

He wore nothing so formal as a tie, but a silk scarf inside the collar of his shirt which made him not only appear tidier, but also in some way gave him a new dignity.

It made Athena find it hard to look at him as she approached the table, but his eyes were on her face and it would have been impossible for her to go anywhere except to his side.

"Dinner is ready," he said speaking in Greek and she answered him in the same language.

"I am very hungry, I hope Madame Argeros will not think I am greedy."

"There is plenty for everyone," Madame said.

She set a dish down on the table and Athena saw that it was the famous *Moussaka* which she had eaten before and which she had learnt varied from place to place and from kitchen to kitchen.

It might be a Greek speciality, but she thought it resembled very closely the Shepherd's Pie that she had eaten so often at home and which in the School-Room always appeared on Monday made from the left-overs of the Sunday joint.

However with Greek olives, herbs, aubergines and various other vegetables added she found Moussaka very delectable and because she was hungry ate without speaking.

Orion filled her glass with the golden wine and by the time they had consumed large portions of baby lamb roasted on the spit the edge of Athena's hunger and, she thought, Orion's too had gone.

They started to talk to the Argeros family who had joined them at the table, but either Nonika or her father kept rising to attend the customers sitting outside the Taverna.

They continually and loudly demanded bottles of wine or cups of coffee, but with the exception of olives and an occasional plate of cheese, they did not ask for food.

Athena commented on this.

"The Greeks eat very late," Orion explained. "Madame Argeros panders to my preference for an early dinner, but if I was not here I doubt if she would begin cooking until it was nearly ten o'clock."

"But they get up very early," Athena answered, remembering that the streets of Greece had been crowded when she had looked out at six or even five o'clock in the morning.

"Every Greek enjoys a long siesta during the hottest time of the day," Orion said, "just as you took yours this afternoon."

"But I did it inadvertently," Athena replied almost defensively.

"Consciously or unconsciously you conformed with the customs of my country," he smiled.

His eyes were on hers as he spoke and she remembered how she had awoken to find him sitting beside her when she had been dreaming that she was flying with the eagles.

She felt herself blush at what she thought he must be thinking and was glad when Madame Argeros broke the tension by saying:

"We have bad news to-day."

"Bad news?" Orion questioned.

"There was trouble at Arachova last night."

Athena knew that Arachova was a small town about four hours from Delphi on the road over the mountains leading to Athens.

It was where the wine came from and the inhabitants wove tufted rugs which were famous all over Greece.

She had been shown several of them when she was in Athens and had made up her mind to buy one because they were so attractive.

"What happened in Arachova?" Orion asked.

"Kazandis was there!"

Orion seemed to stiffen in his seat.

"I thought he was in prison."

"Apparently he escaped," Madame replied. "He swept down on the town last night and although they tried to drive him away he stole a considerable number of things before he left."

"That is serious," Orion remarked.

"Who is Kazandis?" Athena enquired.

"A bandit," Orion answered, "of the type that I was warning you about. He is a dangerous man who is thought to have murdered a number of people in the valleys."

"They should have hanged him when they had the chance," Madame Argeros said shrilly. "No-one can feel safe in their houses when Kazandis is at large."

"The trouble was that no-one would bear witness against him," Orion said. "They were too frightened of the vengeance he would wreak upon them."

He brought his fist down hard on the table making the glasses rattle.

"How could the Military be so stupid as to allow him to escape? He was committed to prison for a long sentence."

"From all I hear there is a great deal of corruption in the State Prisons," Argeros said from the head of the table.

"I have heard that too, but it is difficult to prove," Orion replied.

"There must be something wrong when a man like Kazandis can escape," Madame Argeros said sharply. "He is a menace, and if he has managed to free himself from gaol I am quite certain he will have left a number of dead bodies behind him."

Orion turned towards Athena.

"Now you understand why you should not be travelling alone, especially in this part of the world."

"There are always dragons wherever one may travel," she answered, "but perhaps too there is an Apollo, or maybe a Hermes, to save me from them."

She spoke lightly but Orion's expression was serious.

"I am worried about you," he said in English.

"I shall be all . . . right," she answered.

At the same time, because he was so concerned she felt a little flicker of fear within herself.

Up to now she had not thought there might be any dangers other than being prevented from coming to Delphi.

Now it seemed there were indeed dragons that she had not anticipated, but she thought it very unlikely that she would encounter one.

"The whole trouble with the country is that too much attention is paid to what happens in the city and not enough in the Provinces," Dimitrios Argeros said provocatively.

"That was inevitable while we were a divided nation," Orion replied. "But now we are a Kingdom things should improve, and I understand that representations on that very subject have been made to the King."

"The King!" There was a world of meaning in the way Argeros said it. "He is a good man, but he is not a Greek."

"That is true," Orion agreed.

"Only a Greek can understand Greece," Argeros went on. "Only a Greek can sympathise with us when our crops fail, when the sea does not yield its fish, when the gods withhold the rain, or drown the soil."

Then the arguments started, arguments which Athena thought she had listened to in England, the countryman against the town-dweller, the farmer against the artisan, and all against the Government.

She liked the way each man put his point, concisely and eloquently, and the manner in which as if they fought a duel they tried to make their point and defeat the other with the flash and sparkle of words.

Sometimes Madame Argeros joined in but Nonika listened, wide-eyed, only having to rise to attend to the noisy orders of those outside on the porch.

Finally when the wine and the coffee were finished Orion rose to his feet.

"We agree in principle," he said to his host.

"Which is more than the Government does," Argeros grumbled and Orion laughed.

"Come along, Athena," he said. "You could stay here listening all night to Greek politics, but I doubt if you would be any the wiser at the end of it. The whole trouble with this country is that there is too much talk and not enough 'do'."

He said this as a parting shot at Argeros who laughed and

made a remark that Athena did not understand but which made Orion laugh too.

Then they had left the Taverna behind and were descending the road up which they had climbed earlier in the day.

While they had been eating and talking the sun had sunk and the stars had come out in the sky and with them the moon.

It was not yet full, but there was light enough to see the way.

As they passed the houses of the village and came near to the Sacred Shrine Athena could see that a mist hung over the valley so that the Shining Cliffs seemed to be floating over a vast and mysterious chasm.

Now the broken marble columns and the strange shapes lying among the grasses were haloed with silver and acquired a new form and grace that they had not had before.

It was very silent save for a dog barking far away in the village; Athena could hear the water flowing from the chasm and the air was filled with the fragrance of wild thyme.

In silence she and Orion climbed the broken steps and moved through the long flower-filled grasses towards the Temple of Apollo.

He put his hand under her elbow to help her and with the feeling of his fingers on her bare skin she felt a strange little tremor go through her and she thought perhaps it was because the mystery and darkness of the night was so awe-inspiring.

They climbed until they had passed the columns of Apollo and had reached the theatre above it.

Below them it was possible to make out the complete shape of the Temple and the white stones and columns seemed to make a pattern that Athena had not been able to perceive in the daytime.

Now they shone like crystals and there were strange shadows in the sanctuary which made her feel it was peopled with the priests and pilgrims of the past, and with the presence of the god himself.

Far below she could just make out the sea glimmering through the gap in the great dark mountain rocks.

As she looked the moon came out fuller throwing a shimmering icy lightness over the whole valley, and now it seemed to her that the very air was filled with a mysterious quivering and the beating of silver wings.

A light blinded her eyes so that she felt as if Apollo himself materialised before her and she could see him in all his glory surrounded by stars.

She almost felt as if she could take wing and fly towards him. Then she heard Orion's deep voice speaking for the first time since they had left the Taverna.

"Tell me what you feel."

"It is wonderful! Lovely! So beautiful," Athena murmured almost beneath her breath, "that I want to ... hold the moonlight in my arms. I want to ... kiss it and make it ... mine."

"That is what I want."

Then he turned her round and his lips were on hers.

For a moment Athena was so bemused by her feelings that she could hardly believe that it was Orion kissing her rather than Apollo.

She felt his lips hard and possessive against the softness of her own.

Then as if it was part of the whole magic of the night, the moonlight and the Shining Cliffs, she found herself without conscious volition melt closely against him.

She surrendered her mouth to his, feeling as if everything that was happening was inevitable – pre-ordained and what in the depths of her heart, she had expected.

His arms tightened and now his lips seemed to draw not only her soul from her but also her life itself.

She became one with the moon, the stars and of course Orion.

It was so wonderful that Athena felt as though she was

disembodied, and at the same time the moonlight was not only all around but within her.

It was hers and she held it in her arms and in the innermost sanctuary of her soul.

Time stood still.

She was aware of a rapture and an ecstasy that was not of the world but belonged to Olympus. Orion was not a man but a god, and she was Athena, goddess of love.

How long they stood there it was impossible to know, a century might have passed or more.

Slowly Orion raised his head and looked down at Athena with her eyes shining as they stared up at him, her lips soft and warm from his kisses, and a radiance in her face that gave her a spiritual beauty that was indescribable.

For a moment they looked at each other, then with an inarticulate sound that seemed to come from the very depths of his being he was kissing her again.

Kissing her now demandingly, possessively, until she clung to him even closer, aware of strange sensations within herself which she had not known existed.

Finally when she felt as if he carried her as the eagles had up into the sky so that she no longer had her feet on the ground, he released her so suddenly that she staggered and almost fell.

As he put out his hand to steady her, she sat down on one of the stone seats of the Theatre.

She stared up at him, her fingers entwining themselves as if only by touch could she believe that she was still human, still flesh and blood.

He stood looking at her for a long moment, then sat down beside her.

"You have never been kissed before."

His voice was very deep and moved.

She shook her head. Her voice had died in her throat from the sheer wonder of what she had just experienced.

"Then you know now that this is how a kiss should be, pure and sacred as only the gods understand purity."

Athena did not reply and after a moment he said in what she knew was a different tone:

"This has been a dream, Athena. We both have to go back to reality, but I think neither of us will ever forget."

Athena drew in her breath.

Somehow it seemed to her as if he was speaking to her from very far away and was difficult to understand.

"Y..you are ... going away," she managed to say at length and her voice sounded very unlike her own.

"I am leaving early to-morrow morning," he replied, "before you are awake. But I wanted to say good-bye to you here, for nowhere else would have seemed so right."

There was a silence in which the moonlight shining on the pillars beneath them seemed to look almost like tears. Then Athena said hesitatingly:

"Must ... it be ... good-bye?"

She did not know what she really meant or what alternative she could offer, she only knew that every instinct in her body cried out against losing him, against being separated from the wonder and magic of his lips.

There was a pause. He was looking down into the valley and his clear-cut profile was silhouetted against the broken and moss covered tiers of the theatre, which had once held an enraptured audience.

"This has been a dream, Athena," he said slowly. "A dream sent to us by the gods and I think neither of us could bear to spoil it."

He drew in his breath as he went on:

"It has been a moment of utter perfection; a moment which is engraved on my heart for all time."

"And on ... mine," Athena whispered.

"That is why there is nothing we can say to each other. There is no need for explanations. I could not bear to ask for them – or make them."

She knew what he was trying to say and she accepted that it was inevitable.

They were strangers, and because they had met in the

abode of gods they had for a moment assumed a god-like isolation from the rest of their lives.

They had been swept away from the normal into a spiritual existence which neither of them had ever known before. They had been disembodied, touched with the divinity of the gods themselves and for one ecstatic moment had become divine.

Now they must face reality and Athena wished that she could have died while his lips were on hers.

Then she would have achieved immortality: there would have been no problems, no difficulties, no human needs to which she must return.

She wanted to cry out at the pain of relinquishing the wonder she had known in Orion's arms, then to weep perhaps with despair. But because she knew that nothing she could say could alter their destiny she kept silent.

"There is no need for me to tell you that this is something which has never happened to me before in my life," Orion was saying, "and which I am certain will never happen again. You were rightly named, Athena, you are the goddess of love and you have brought me love which I believed existed but had never found."

"That is how ... love should ... be," Athena murmured.

"That is why the pilgrims came here," he said. "That is why there are pilgrims all over the world seeking love, the love which has led, guided and inspired man since the beginning of time."

"It was the ... love they gave ... Apollo," Athena said softly.

"And the love Athena gave to them."

They sat looking down at the ruined Temple and the valley beyond it and although he was not touching her Athena felt as if she was still in his arms.

Finally with a sigh he rose to his feet.

"I must take you back."

She rose too to stand looking at him, her face raised to his, the moonlight shining in her eyes.

He knew without words what she asked and what she wanted of him and he said quietly:

"I will not kiss you again because after to-night our paths will never cross each other's and I dare not repeat that moment when we both reached the heights of bliss and were one with the gods."

Athena's eyes were on his and he looked at her as if he was spellbound and he could not look away.

"I am after all only a man," he said, "and if as a man I kissed you again I might try to change the pattern of our lives, and that would be a mistake."

Athena wanted to protest, wanted to tell him that she wanted above all things, the pattern of her life to be changed, to be with him, to have him kiss her and that nothing else was of any consequence in the whole world.

"You are lovely!" he said hoarsely, "more lovely than I believed any woman could be. That is why, having known you, I am convinced that no other woman will ever matter to me again."

Athena felt her heart leap.

It was like a streak of joy running through her and he must have seen it in her eyes, for almost as if she had spoken he said firmly:

"No! No, Athena!"

Then he turned and walked back down the twisting stone path that led to the road.

After a moment she followed him because there was nothing else she could do.

As she went, finding it difficult at times to keep her balance without his supporting hand, she felt that he would disappear away from her into the shadows so that she would never find him.

"Perhaps," she thought wildly, "he never existed. Perhaps he is part of my dreams or perhaps he is in fact not human, but has come from the constellation of stars whose name he bears."

But he was waiting for her when she reached the road.

She thought his expression was stern and that his jaw was set so that it seemed as if he had already left her and she was alone as she had been alone before they met.

They walked up the road without speaking, past the shuttered village, and although light gleamed in many of the windows there was a silence that seemed now to Athena not magical, but oppressive.

Several dogs barked as they passed and Athena felt that they were hostile because she was an intruder and did not belong.

After the steep climb to the Taverna, they could see the lights glowing golden from its windows. But the porch was empty and the old men had gone home.

The chairs were stacked tidily on the tables as Orion opened the door into the house. The warmth of the kitchen after the cold of the moonlight was almost like a shock.

Madame Argeros and her husband were sitting at the table. He was smoking and they each had a cup of coffee in front of them, but there was no sign of Nonika.

Madame smiled as they entered.

"You are back!" she exclaimed. "That is good. I have kept some coffee warm for you."

"How kind of you, Madame," Orion said conventionally.

Athena moved towards the other door which led to the stairs.

"I think I will go to bed," she said in a voice which sounded strangled in her throat.

"You will not have some coffee?" Madame Argeros asked.

"No ... thank you ... I am tired ... it has been a ... long day."

She did not look at Orion although she was vividly conscious that he had walked to the table. He pulled out a chair and sat down opposite Dimitrios Argeros.

She wanted to stay beside him. She wanted to eke out the last minutes that she could be with him, but she felt it might somehow spoil the wonder of all they had experienced.

The glory of his kiss still pulsated within her, even while she knew inevitably the rapture of it was fading.

Soon it would be gone and she felt despairingly that there would be nothing but an aching void that would be with her all the rest of her life.

"We wish you good-night," Madame said. "May you sleep well."

"Thank you," Athena answered.

Then as she would have turned away the door of the Taverna was flung violently open.

The noise of it made them all turn instinctively to see entering the kitchen a huge man.

He was wearing a short sheep-skin coat with a fur hat set jauntily on the side of his head.

He was very dark with bushy eye-brows, a long curling moustache, the ends of it reaching almost to his chin where they had been curled fastidiously.

There was a pistol stuck in his belt, besides a long knife, and as his black eyes looked around the kitchen searchingly and somehow insolently Madame Argeros gave a scream.

"Kazandis!"

"Yes, Kazandis," the Bandit answered. "Are you surprised to see me? You should have expected me, for where else in these regions can I get better food?"

He walked forward as he spoke and pulling out a chair from the table sat down at the end of it.

"I want food," he said, "money and..."

He paused for a moment and he stared towards Athena.

Mesmerized she stood in the open doorway, her hair golden in the light from the lamp, her skin very white against the dark walls of the kitchen.

She felt as Kazandis looked at her that somehow he stripped her naked and her heart gave a frightened leap as he finished his sentence.

"... and a woman!"

There was silence in the kitchen, then Orion rose to his feet.

Swiftly as he moved the Bandit was swifter.

He drew the pistol from his belt and pointed it at him.

"Any opposition from you," he said, "and not only you will die but also the Argeros' and anyone else who interferes with me!"

"You shall have your food," Madame interrupted. "You are fortunate there is some left. Here is wine."

She set a bottle down on the table with a bang as she spoke and walked towards the stove. No-one else moved. Then slowly, without the impetuosity he had shown the first time, Orion rose.

"Madame will provide you with your needs," he said, "and I shall make no effort to interfere. But this woman is my wife. We have not been married long, but she is with child."

The Bandit looked across the room at Athena and at the slimness of her figure.

"That is why she is retiring to bed," Orion said firmly. "Do you understand?"

The Bandit looked at him as if to make certain he was telling the truth. Orion's eyes met his fairly and squarely.

After a moment he grunted, poured out a glass of wine and swilled it down without speaking.

Orion crossed the room, put his arm around Athena and took her through the door which led to the stairs. He deliberately left it open as if to let the Bandit see that they were not escaping.

"Go up to bed and lock your door. You will be quite safe," he said in English.

"You are ... sure?"

Athena was trembling.

"Quite sure," he answered.

He did not touch her, but he watched her as she climbed the stairs, and heard her go into the room overhead.

There was no lock on the door, but there was a bolt made of wood and Athena pushed it into place.

The shutters over the window were closed and she made no effort to open them, she could not bear to look at the moonlight. Nonika had left a rush candle burning and by the light of it Athena undressed and got into bed.

She thought it would be impossible to think of anything but the Bandit sitting downstairs, but although she could hear the murmur of their voices she began to relive the moment when Orion had kissed her in the Sacred Shrine.

With her eyes closed she could still see the outline of the Temple, the silver mist in the valley and the glimmer of the sea.

It all seemed to glow within her with the shining light which she knew came from Apollo himself.

It was perfect, it was wonderful, and even now she could hardly believe that her spirit, having soared to the Heavens in Orion's arms, was back within the confines of her body.

She would never see him again. He was leaving her, as strangely and mysteriously as he had come. Orion – the stranger who was no longer a stranger but a part of herself.

She felt cold with the pain and misery of it. She wanted him, wanted him with an intensity that was violent.

How could she lose him? How could she forget the moment when she gave herself to him completely and absolutely, keeping back nothing, merging her whole being into his until they were one person?

She wanted to cry out in despair, and yet her eyes were dry and she knew there were no words by which she could express her feelings, not even to him.

For one moment of her life she had been transformed from a conventional English girl into, as he had said, the goddess of love.

Now when he left her, she would return to what she had been before except that nothing could ever be the same again.

Having once touched the very fount of happiness and of

ecstasy, having once known the rapture of the initiated into the mysteries of the gods, how could she return to ordinary life?

How could she face commonplace people and the thought of living perhaps three-score-years-and-ten without the man she loved?

Put into words it seemed incredible.

How could she love a man she had never met until this afternoon? Yet she knew inexorably and irrefutably that this, as Orion had said, was the love that all men sought.

Journeying as pilgrims, following twisting philosophies and innumerable religions they sought in their souls what she and Orion had captured in one immortal moment on the broken steps of the theatre.

"I love him!"

She said the words to herself, and they seemed to be emblazoned across the darkness in letters of fire.

"I love him! I love him! He is the only person who understands."

To anyone else the story would sound ridiculous: they would laugh and tell her she was just an imaginative, romantic girl, carried away by the moonlight.

But Athena knew it was something fundamental and eternal.

It was soul reaching out to soul, spirit reaching out to spirit, a woman finding the man who was hers and to whom she had belonged from the beginning of creation.

This was love, this was the fate which drew two people to each other, so that whatever the appearances against it they became one in the real and spiritual sense of the word.

"When Orion leaves to-morrow he takes my heart with him," Athena whispered to the darkness.

A long time later she heard him coming up the stairs.

There was silence below and she guessed that the Bandit must have gone, doubtless taking with him all the money the Argeros' had in the house and anything else of value he fancied.

As Orion reached the landing and opened the door of his room she fancied that he stood for a moment listening as if to ascertain that she was all right.

She wanted to cry out to him, but she knew that that was something he did not want – and anyway modesty kept her silent.

Orion went into the other room and shut the door.

She heard him walking about on the uncarpeted floor then she heard the bed move beneath him.

She wondered what he looked like asleep, perhaps younger and gentler, and not so overwhelmingly masculine as he had looked when his deep-set eyes sought hers and she felt shy yet excited by the expression in them.

"I love him! I love him!" Athena whispered to herself.

She knew that he intended to rise early in the morning before she was awake, but she was sure that after all that had happened she would be unable to sleep, and if he made the slightest sound she would hear it.

It would be a worse agony than anything she could imagine to hear him going downstairs and leaving the house without saying good-bye.

And yet what could they say to each other that had not already been said?

It would be a bathos that was unthinkable to shake hands or even to kiss each other perfunctorily after what had happened at the shrine.

No – there would be nothing she could do but listen to him leaving, and know that after he had gone she must return to the world from which she had escaped for one brief ecstatic day.

"However long I live I shall never be able to love anyone else," Athena thought.

Deep in her thoughts she was vaguely aware of a scrabbling sound against the wall of the house.

She had not really noticed it, but now she distinctly heard a footstep overhead.

It was not loud, and yet it was followed by another one,

and she looked up apprehensively in the darkness at the ceiling.

Again she heard a noise and now with a sudden shock of terror she knew what it was.

Someone was on the roof over her head and it was not difficult to guess the intruder's identity. He was obviously trying to open the trap-door which was built in most flat-roofed houses to let in the cool night air when the weather was hot.

Athena sat up in bed.

It was Kazandis who was overhead – and she knew that he intended to enter her room from the roof above.

He would know where she was sleeping because he would have heard her moving about when she went to bed, and although he had pretended to accept Orion's story that she was his wife and with child it was doubtful if he had been deceived.

Terror-stricken, she realised that the trap-door in the roof was opening.

It was obviously stiff through not having been used since last year, but although she could not see in the darkness she felt that strong fingers were already raising it.

There was a creaking noise, then a faint light above her!

With a cry like a frightened animal Athena jumped out of bed.

She ran across the room and groped with frantic, trembling fingers for the bolt on the door.

As she found it she heard the trap door fall back on to the roof and felt the night air on her face.

Then she pulled the door open, ran across the landing and grasped the handle of Orion's door.

It turned, and unable to breathe from sheer terror Athena let herself in.

Chapter Four

Orion had opened his shutters when he went to bed, and in the moonlight flooding into the room he could see, as he sat up, Athena at the door.

She turned to push in the bolt which was similar to the one on the door of her bed-room, then frantically she ran across the room towards him.

"What is the matter? What has happened?" he asked.

Without thinking she threw herself against him and his arms went round her.

"Th..that man," she managed to gasp, "he is ... getting into my bed-room f..from the...roof."

Orion's arms tightened for a moment. Then he said quietly:

"Shut your eyes. I am going to get out of bed."

He moved as he spoke, and hardly understanding what was happening Athena had a glimpse of his body, slim, athletically muscled, silver in the moonlight, and realised he was naked.

Hastily she covered her face with her hands.

She sat trembling on the bed, her back towards him until, as he moved about, he said:

"Get into the bed. I will not let him touch you."

Fearfully she turned her head to see that Orion dressed in his trousers and shirt was pulling the furniture in front of the door.

Automatically, still too bemused really to know what she was doing, she got into the bed as he had ordered and pulled the sheet over her.

It was a large bed, larger than the one in her room, but

she sat upright watching Orion dragging first the chest-of-drawers, then a table and various other pieces of furniture in front of the door, piling them up one upon the other.

He made a considerable noise while he was doing it, and she thought that if Kazandis was by this time in her bed-room he must realise what was happening.

She knew now that Orion had gambled on the Bandit respecting her because he had said she was not only a married woman but also carrying a child.

Perhaps he had believed, as she did, the age-old saying of the Ancient Greeks that the three most beautiful things in the world were a ship in full sail, a cornfield blowing in the wind, and a woman with child.

He had been mistaken.

Kazandis respected nothing and nobody, and Athena trembled as she thought that if she had been asleep he would have entered her bed-room and been beside her before she was aware of his presence.

Then there would have been no escape.

Even now when she thought of the huge man with his pistol and his knife and the lustful expression in his eyes she could not be sure she was free of him.

She looked up at the ceiling trying to see if there was a trap-door to the roof in Orion's room as there had been in hers.

Then she realised that even if there were Kazandis would not have risked entering the room by such a method when there was a man in it.

He would be too vulnerable to assault as he descended, for there would be no other way of coming down except feet first.

Then even as she thought about it she heard a heavy footstep on the landing outside.

Kazandis must have got into her bed-room as he intended only to find that his prey had flown.

He would have guessed where she had gone and he would know now that he had been right in assuming that Orion had lied to him when he said they were man and wife.

Athena held her breath, and she fancied that Orion standing back a little way from the door and listening was also holding his.

She noticed that while he had pulled most of the furniture against the door there was a strongly made wooden chair beside him.

She guessed he intended if necessary to use this as a weapon and thought despairingly that although it might prove effective against an un-armed man, it would be useless against a bullet from a pistol with which Kazandis was doubtless an expert.

There was no sound of movement outside on the landing, and yet he was certainly there.

It was almost as if they could hear him breathing, almost as if they could see, mentally, his brain working, wondering if he should force his way into the room and overpower Orion, which he could be quite capable of doing, and then take Athena as he wished to do.

It must have been only a few seconds, but it seemed to Athena as if hours ticked by.

She was conscious only of the frenzied beating of her heart and the straining of her ears.

Then abruptly, unexpectedly, they heard Kazandis stump noisily down the stairs.

It was as if by the very noise he made he defied them and refused to acknowledge defeat.

They heard him fling open the door leading into the kitchen, cross the room beneath and let himself out of the Taverna, slamming the door behind him.

Athena felt her whole body relax and it was almost painful because the tension had been so strained.

Now Orion turned to face her and she saw in the moonlight that he was smiling.

"He has gone."

He came across the room towards her and sat down on the bed facing her, his eyes taking in the thin white muslin nightgown she was wearing, trimmed with lace, her fair hair falling over her shoulders and her eyes wide and frightened, looking into his.

"You are safe, Athena," he said again as if she had not understood. "He has gone."

"Suppose he ... comes back?" she whispered.

"He will not. I should have anticipated that something like this would happen and I apologise for not taking better care of you."

"It was not your ... fault," Athena said. "I thought he ... believed you."

"I hoped he did, but marriage vows mean nothing to Kazandis and he has a reputation with women as with everything else."

"Can there be ... women who like a man ... like that?" Athena asked. Then she added wonderingly, "I did not ... understand that men could ... feel that way."

"About what?" Orion asked.

She was silent for a moment, then said in a voice he could hardly hear:

"He ... asked for food and a ... woman as if they were the ... same kind of thing."

There was something so shocked in the tone of her voice that Orion reached out and put his hand over hers.

"Forget it," he said. "In the sheltered life I imagine you have led and will continue to lead when you go home you are never likely to meet another man like Kazandis. But you see, I was right in warning you that you must take care of yourself."

Athena drew in her breath.

"If ... you had ... not been ... there ...' she whispered.

"But I was here," Orion said firmly. "Forget it, Athena, it is something that might happen once in a million times, and then only to someone like yourself who has run away from those who are looking after her."

He paused before he asked:

"You have run away, have you not?"

Athena's eyes flickered and she looked down.

"Yes," she admitted after a moment.

"I can understand your wanting to go to Delphi alone," he said. "The presence of other people can spoil such an unforgettable experience as a first visit to the Shrine. At the same time you are too beautiful, Athena, to take chances with yourself."

There was a note in his voice which made her glance up at him quickly, and then it was impossible to look away.

For a moment they both stared at each other and Athena knew that something magnetic passed between them and she felt as if once again she was in his arms and his lips were on hers.

Abruptly Orion rose to his feet.

"I know you will not wish to go back to your own room," he said, "so we will change places."

Without thinking Athena put out her hands towards him.

"No ... do not ... leave me," she begged. "Please ... do not ... leave me."

She did not realise what she was asking, she only knew the fear of what had happened swept over her, and her whole body shrank from being alone and from the fear that however securely Orion might fasten the door Kazandis would somehow reach her.

There were two windows in this room and she was sure there was also a trap-door in the ceiling.

In her imagination she could almost see Kazandis killing Orion while he slept. Then there would be no-one to protect her or to prevent him from battering down the door and coming to her if he wished to do so.

It was the cry of a frightened child as she repeated:

'I ... cannot be alone ... I could not ... bear it."

Orion walked to the window to stand in the moonlight. She could see his profile with its perfect Greek features etched against the lintel and she thought, as she had thought before, that no man could be so handsome or indeed so irresistible.

"I understand what you are feeling, Athena," he said after a moment, and she thought that his voice was deliberately controlled. "So you will stay here and I will stay with you, but you must understand that it will be difficult for me and I dare not touch you."

"Why?" Athena whispered.

She felt as if his words conjured up an enchantment that crept over her insidiously like a warm wave.

Now she was trembling, but not with fear.

She felt the same excitement she had felt when he kissed her and carried her up into the sky, where they had ceased to be human beings and had become gods.

"You know the answer to that," Orion answered harshly. "We said good-bye to each other, Athena. It is something we had to do because you have your life to live and I have mine. I had steeled myself not to see you again."

He sounded reproachful and Athena replied:

"I am ... sorry."

She knew as she spoke that she was nothing of the sort, since now that the horror that had driven her to him was over, he was there.

She could look at him, she could listen to his voice even if it were only for a short time until once again they must leave each other.

"We can mean – nothing to each other in the future," Orion went on almost as if he spoke to himself, "and this is only prolonging the agony for me, if not for you."

It was a worse agony for her than he imagined, she thought.

Whatever the responsibilities to which he had to return, he did not understand that she had to go back to Mikis to tell the Prince that she would not marry him, to face her Aunt's anger and undoubtedly his.

She had thought before she came to Delphi that it would

be very difficult, creating arguments and a situation with which she felt very inadequate to cope.

But now, having met Orion, she knew that not only to marry a man she did not love was impossible but whatever happened she would never now consent to marry the Prince.

Perhaps, she thought to herself, her bravery when she left the Palace had been superficial, and if the Prince had proved as pleasant and as charming as everybody averred she might have allowed herself to give in to the pressure that would undoubtedly have been put upon her.

It would be, Athena was well aware, ignominious and humiliating to return to England unmarried.

She would have to make explanations not only to her family but also to those relatives and friends who had been let in on the secret of what her journey to Athens actually entailed.

There was also the Greek Ambassador and members of his staff who had come to Wadebridge Castle to discuss the proposals with her father and grandmother.

At the thought of the Dowager Marchioness Athena felt much more apprehensive than she did in regard to the rest of her family.

Her grandmother had always meant so much to her. She had taken her mother's place after she had died, and she had adored her from the moment she was old enough to recognise anyone.

The Dowager Marchioness was now old and in ill health, and Athena feared that after setting her heart on arranging this marriage between the Prince of her House and her favourite grandchild, to learn that her arrangements had failed would be almost like a death-blow.

"I cannot help it," Athena thought. "Much as I love Grandmama I cannot do as she wishes, not after having met Orion and learning what love between two people really means."

This was not the bloodless comradeship between a man and a woman who had common interests or who were prepared, because they met more or less on equal terms, to find friendship and perhaps even a sexual satisfaction in each other.

What she felt for Orion was love.

She looked at him across the room and she thought that his face shone with a light that was echoed in her own.

Together they had found perfect love, together they had penetrated the mystic innermost shrine of life itself.

How could either of them afterwards ever be satisfied with second best?

"I shall never marry," Athena thought wildly, and remembered how often she had been told that marriage meant more to a woman than to a man.

Orion would find himself a wife — for all she knew he might have one already and she would merely remain in his mind as a moment of enchantment.

Perhaps he would remember her when the moon was full or when he came to Delphi again.

She felt as if her whole body cried out in protest, and yet what could she do?

As if with an effort Orion turned from the window.

"You must rest," he said. "Lie down, Athena, and try to go to sleep. You are quite safe while I am here and I am almost certain that we shall hear no more of Kazandis."

He paused to add:

"He has taken a large sum of money from Argeros, and as his action will doubtless be reported to the Military as will his robbery of last night at Arachova he will know that the soldiers are looking for him and will keep away from this region for some time."

Athena knew that he was talking to reassure her.

Looking round the bare room she said:

"What will ... you do?"

"I am going to take one of the pillows from the bed," Orion said, "and there is a blanket in the cupboard. I promise you I shall be quite comfortable on the floor. I have slept in worse places and everything in the Taverna is very clean."

"I... I would not wish you to be... uncomfortable. If you want to go to my room I will try to be... brave and you could leave the doors open so that you will hear if I... called out to you."

"Did you call or scream when you knew Kazandis was breaking into your room from the roof?" Orion enquired.

She did not answer and he smiled.

"I know exactly what happened. Your voice died in your throat. It is what happens to most people when they are really afraid."

He moved around to the other side of the bed and picked up a pillow.

"So we will do things my way, Athena. Lie down and try to relax. You have had a long day and I feel quite certain you will sleep."

"And... you?"

"I am used to going without sleep," he answered, "and if I do doze off, it will be with one eye open, like wild animals who are seldom taken by surprise."

He walked across the room with the pillow in his hand and she had the feeling that he deliberately did not look at her when he came to the bed.

There was a cupboard on the opposite wall and on a shelf at the top of it was a folded blanket.

Orion drew it out and put it down on the floor in a patch of silvery light made by the moon-beams.

"Now you can see me," he said, "and you will not feel afraid. Good-night, Athena. Try to sleep."

"You will not... go in the... morning without... telling me?" she pleaded.

"I suspect that however carefully I move you will hear me," he answered, "but I shall be leaving very early. My horse has been ordered and to-night I told the man who brought you from Itea that you would be leaving at about seven o'clock. Madame Argeros will give you breakfast before you go."

He had arranged everything, Athena thought despairingly, and felt as if he almost told her what she must do for the rest of her life.

She wondered what he would say if she confided in him.

Would he, because he was Greek, tell her that her duty lay in marrying the Prince? Would his patriotism mean more to him than his feelings for her?

She could not believe that any man feeling as he must have felt when he swept her up to the stars would wish to hand her over tamely to another man who might teach her to love him.

And yet after all what did she know about Orion? They had talked together for a few brief hours.

Yet they had found the secret of eternity together and that meant more than a lifetime of knowledge.

"Shall I tell him?" Athena asked herself.

Then she thought there was really no point. He had already given her the answer to her problem and as far as she was concerned it was "no".

It was not only that she knew she could not bear another man to touch her; it would also be intolerable to live in Greece with the knowledge that once she was married somehow, by some chance, she might encounter Orion again.

She knew it would be impossible not to look for him in every crowd, at every party, in every street.

She would be searching the faces of every man she saw for those perfect features, for that slim, athletic body, for the curve of his dark head.

And if they did meet – what then?

She had no idea what he did. All she knew with certainty was that he was the most cultured and civilised man she had ever met.

That was not to say that he might not live in very humble circumstances while she ... she would be a Princess!

"I must go away," Athena thought. "I must return to

England and forget there was ever such a country as Greece and one man who means to me everything that was the splendour, the beauty and the inspiration of the past."

Orion had arranged his hard bed to his satisfaction and now he said:

"You are not lying down, Athena, as I told you to do. Shut your eyes and think of all the happiness we have known to-day. Forget everything else."

He was still thinking that she was afraid, Athena knew. But her thoughts were far away from Kazandis, and instead she was thinking only of Orion and what it would mean to lose him.

But because of the note of authority in his voice she did as he told her. She lay down, pulling the sheet over her shoulders and turning her cheek against the soft pillow.

"Good-night, Athena," Orion said as he lay down on the floor.

"Will you ... always remember to-day?" she asked softly.

"You know the answer to that question," he replied. "It would be impossible for me ever to forget."

His words were somehow comforting but she wanted to ask him so much more. Yet instinctively she knew that if she did he would not give her the right answers.

All the time they had been together she had known without being told in words that there was a deep reserve about him and it was that reserve which she knew now was like an impregnable wall between them.

And after all, what could she suggest?

That they should meet after she returned to the Palace? That was impossible!

That she should not return to the Palace?

Athena knew in her heart that was what she wanted!

She wanted Orion to ask her to stay with him and, unbelievable though it seemed, she knew what her answer would be.

Whatever the hardships she might encounter, whatever the heart-breaks, if they came, it would be worth everything to be with him if only for a year, a month, a week, any time however short, so that their love would be complete.

How strange it was, Athena thought, that while most people looked forward to living perhaps seventy years, all she wanted to live was just one moment of time however brief in the arms of one man.

It was difficult to express even to herself, but she knew that the life that had been hers for eighteen years had not been the fulfilment of everything of which she was capable.

There was no reason to think, however many years she lived in the future, that they would be any different.

In those minutes, when Orion kissed her and she had experienced a wonder and glory that was not of this world, she had lived – perhaps a whole lifetime – to the fullest of what any man or woman was capable and still remain human.

"How can I lose it? How can I let it go?" she asked herself and knew there was no answer.

Athena was very innocent, but she could not help feeling that any other man in the world in the situation in which she was now would not be lying on the floor on the other side of the room but beside her.

She attracted Orion, he felt about her as she felt about him, and yet deliberately he would not accept the fact that she was all too willing to surrender herself. He would not allow his desires to overthrow the conviction of his mind.

She respected him for it as she knew he would respect her, and yet her whole being wanted him so insistently, so violently, that only a lifetime of self-control prevented Athena from running to lie down beside him.

She wanted to feel herself close against him, she wanted to find in his arms not only the wonder and the glory of love but the protection and the sense of safety which she knew only he could give her.

She felt as if her whole heart cried out to him to understand.

She dared not put what she was feeling into words, and although she knew he was not asleep he did not speak to her again.

Slowly the hours of the night passed, the moonlight gradually began to fade and the silver light was no longer so intense in the little room.

It was then, just before dawn came, that Athena knew Orion was asleep.

For the first time she heard his even breathing and she wondered if any two people had ever spent a stranger night, both needing each other, both awake and both respecting a silent separation that was self-imposed.

"I love him!" Athena thought to herself. "I love him so completely and intensely that even if he wishes to crucify me, as indeed he is doing, I will obey him and do what he wants."

"I will go back," she told herself.

Because she had known Orion, she would face all the difficulties and all the unpleasantness that awaited her with a courage and a self-control which he himself would show in such circumstances.

She would be quite firm – she would promise the Prince large sums of money for the poor of Parnassus.

She had learnt that the whole country was in desperate need of money, suffering from centuries of crippling taxes levied by the Turks and now by the King.

It would not be like accepting the money for himself, and she was certain she could give it to him in such a way that he would not feel humiliated by her generosity.

Then she would go home.

She had no wish to see Athens again; she had no wish to see any other part of Greece.

She just wanted to return in an English ship to the quiet life of Wadebridge Castle.

She knew her father liked having her there with him and she would devote herself to him for the rest of his life.

They would ride together, hunt in the winter, and now that she was old enough she would play hostess instead of her grandmother.

Although she supposed there would be men who would want to make love to her and to marry her, she knew it would be impossible to accept them.

"I shall be dedicated to an ideal," she told herself a little bitterly, "and ideals can be very ... cold and ... lonely ... especially when one grows ... old."

She would fill her days, she would make certain of that. Only as far as her heart was concerned it had been given to one man and it would be impossible for her to give it to any other.

She thought of the many orphanages that her father had on his enormous Estate.

Perhaps when he died, Athena thought, there would be a child to whom she would take a fancy and whom she could adopt.

Anyway there would be plenty of children for her to spend her huge fortune on and England would benefit instead of Greece.

It was easy to plan, but as she sat up very, very carefully so as not by a sudden movement to awaken Orion, she could see him in the gradually lightening sky, lying fast asleep.

Lying on his back with his shirt open nearly to the waist he looked, Athena thought, like a fallen god, perhaps like one of the statues that had once stood in Delphi and which Nero had carried away to Rome.

She had also meant to go to Rome, but now she knew that was another place that was barred to her.

How could she bear to find carved in marble or cast in bronze the man she had known as a living, pulsating being who had sent her blood racing through her veins?

"If I were an artist," Athena thought, "I would try to draw him as he is now. Then when I felt unhappy and miserable I could look at the sketch and remember what he meant to me."

But she knew there was no need for a drawing, a painting or even a sculpture.

Each line of Orion's face was indelibly etched in her mind and she knew that every time she shut her eyes and thought of him he would be there in her consciousness.

"I love you! I love you!" Athena thought looking at him. "Wherever you go, wherever you may be, my love will be with you, protecting you, keeping you, perhaps inspiring you, even if you are unaware of it."

If one believed in prayer, she thought, one must also believe in thought-transference: her prayers and thoughts and living sparks from within herself would wing out across the sea towards Orion and find him.

They would form an aura of protection around him, and perhaps because of it the light that she sensed came from him would bring inspiration and help to all those with whom he came into contact.

"If that is all I can do for you, my beloved," Athena told him silently, "then at least it will be some small way by which I can express my love."

She sat looking at him as the room grew lighter and lighter.

When the first rays of the sun appeared over the horizon suddenly there was a golden glow and the whole room was transformed.

It was then that Orion awoke.

He opened his eyes and sat up abruptly and saw that Athena was looking at him.

"I have been asleep."

"You did not sleep for a very long time," she answered.

"It must be late!" he exclaimed, "and I meant to leave early."

"Does it matter so ... tremendously?"

"I did not mean to see you again."

"But that was ... impossible: you could not have ... left without ... waking me."

"Then as I am so late," Orion said, "I will see you off first. I want to make sure that you are safe, and perhaps that is what I should have arranged in the first place."

He was trying to speak in an ordinary, matter-of-fact manner, and she knew that having looked at her once he deliberately looked away and did not glance again in her direction.

Now he started to move the furniture from the door, putting it back in the places where it stood normally.

After he had finished he walked onto the landing and crossed into her room; she knew that he was satisfying himself that it was safe for her to go there.

He came back into the bed-room.

"I am going downstairs to wash and shave," he said, "and as I am sure Madame Argeros will be awake by now I will order breakfast for both of us. I will also see that your horse is ready for you when you have eaten."

"Thank you," Athena said.

She knew he had taken charge and there was nothing for her to do except to obey his orders.

Orion turned towards the door, then as he reached it he looked back at Athena as he had not done since the first moment of waking.

"You are very beautiful in the morning," he said in a deep voice. "You look like Persephone must have done when she came back from the darkest bowels of the earth to bring spring and hope to mankind."

His eyes seemed to take in everything about her, the soft outline of her breasts beneath the thin nightgown, the gold of her hair falling over her shoulders, the light in her grey eyes which seemed to hold the reflection of the sunlight.

Then he was gone and she heard him clattering down the stairs and a moment later his voice talking to Madame Argeros.

She got out of bed and went to her own room.

She washed in cold water which was no hardship as she realised that soon the sun would be very hot.

She dressed herself and because she knew Orion liked her without a bonnet she decided to carry hers as she had done the day before.

Then she packed her nightgown and all the small things she had brought with her in her Greek bag, stuffing her shawl on the top of them.

She glanced round the room to see that she had forgotten nothing, then for the first time glanced up apprehensively at the trap-door in the ceiling.

It was open and she could see the sky through it.

It was a large aperture and now she saw as she had not noticed before that in one corner of the room there was a ladder which was obviously used in the great heat of the summer by those who wished to sleep on the roof as many Greeks did.

She felt herself shiver as she thought of Kazandis letting himself down into her room.

They had been lucky that he had not forced the issue once he knew where she had gone and sought her across the landing.

She could not have borne, she thought, to watch a fight between Orion and that great hulking Bandit with his huge body and evil eyes.

Of one thing she was quite certain, that he would not have fought fairly and he would undoubtedly have been prepared to fire his pistol and murder Orion if it suited him.

Because the mere thought of what might have happened made her shiver and because above all things she wanted to be with Orion again Athena ran down the stairs.

He was sitting at the table in the kitchen and Madame Argeros was cooking at the stove.

"Good-morning," Madame said as Athena appeared. "Because you are here Orion has asked for an English breakfast and the eggs are ready."

"I am hungry enough to eat a dozen," Orion smiled.

He had risen as he spoke and pulled out a chair so that Athena could sit next to him.

"There's not a dozen," Madame replied, "so you'll have to make do with bacon from the pig we killed only a few weeks ago – and very good it has proved."

"Even Kazandis admitted you had the best food in the whole region," Orion said.

"Kazandis! Don't speak of the man," Madame said bitterly. "He has taken all our money. I warned Dimitrios only yesterday that we had too much in the house, but what man ever listens until it's too late?"

"I am so sorry for you, Madame," Athena said. "You must tell me what I owe you for staying here last night."

"You owe me nothing," Madame said almost sharply. "You are a friend of Orion's, and that is enough. We are not so poverty-stricken – Kazandis or not – that we have to take from our friends."

"But ... I cannot let you ..." Athena began only to feel Orion's hand on her arm.

She looked at him in perplexity; but he shook his head and she understood that she must accept Madame's gesture of generosity and not argue about it.

"It is kind of you," Athena said, "and thank you very much."

But she felt as if she must do something for them and so she said:

"As it is going to be very hot to-day I shall not need my shawl and I wonder if I might leave it for Nonika as she was kind enough to give up her room, and I am sure she will find it useful."

She drew the shawl as she spoke from her bag and remembered that it had in fact been an expensive purchase and had come from Bond Street.

Madame's face softened.

"That would be very kind," she said. "Nonika is collecting things for her trousseau, but for all Greek girls, as things are expensive, it takes a long time and the shawl will therefore be most acceptable."

"Then I am very glad for her to have it," Athena said.

She glanced at Orion as she spoke, hoping that he approved, and knew by his smile and the expression in his eyes that he did.

She felt a warm feeling within her because he was pleased with her, but when she looked at him he looked away and she knew that their parting was near and he was as conscious of it as she was.

Their eggs and bacon were set down in front of them. There was hot coffee, crisp bread and honey which Orion explained came from the bees around Delphi.

"Perhaps they are specially sanctified," he said, "for I always think that the honey here is the most delicious in Greece, although quite a number of my countrymen will tell me I am mistaken."

"Does honey differ in flavour from province to province?" Athena asked.

"Yes, it does," Madame exclaimed before he could speak, "and perhaps the honey from Mount Olympus is the best of all."

"I still continue to disagree with you, Madame," Orion said helping himself to another spoonful.

"You are prejudiced!" Madame Argeros laughed, "but as long as you go on thinking that we have the best, I for one am satisfied."

"Could you ever question it?" he asked.

They finished their breakfast and now Dimitrios Argeros appeared in the doorway to say that their horses were waiting outside.

Athena rose to her feet.

"You are not going in the same direction as I am?" she asked.

He shook his head.

"No. I am riding home over the mountains," he replied,

"but I have already spoken to Spiros which, by the way, is the name of the man who brought you here, and he will take very good care of you – as you must take care of yourself."

He spoke the last words in English in a low voice, and Athena looked up at him and for a moment they were both very still.

He walked towards the door.

Athena thanked Madame Argeros for her kindness, then followed him.

Outside their two horses were waiting and she saw that Orion's was very different from the animal that had brought her up from Itea.

His was a black stallion, extremely high-spirited, and the man who was holding it was having some difficulty in keeping it under control.

It was plunging and bucking and it seemed doubtful that his hold on the bridle would be effective.

"Better not waste much time in mounting that animal," Dimitrios Argeros said. "I hear it nearly kicked a stable down during the night."

"He needs exercise and it is his way of telling me that I have stayed here for too long."

"It has been our gain," Dimitrios Argeros said with surprising eloquence for him. "Come again soon, Orion. You are always welcome – you know that."

"Thank you," Orion replied.

Then as he held out his hand his horse gave another terrific plunge and nearly swept the man holding the bridle off his feet.

"You had best go," Athena said hastily. "There is no hurry for me."

"Perhaps you are right."

He looked at her for a moment, but did not attempt to take her hand. Then as if he had no words in which to express himself he moved away and with surprising ease swung himself into the saddle of the plunging and bucking stallion.

Almost immediately it seemed the animal knew that his master had taken control, and although he fidgeted he no longer proved to be so obstreperous.

Then, as if he was as eager as the horse he was riding to be gone, Orion turned and started to descend the steep road towards the village.

Athena felt as if she could not bear to watch him go and went towards her own horse.

A line written by Lord Byron was ringing in her ears.

"Gone shimmering through the dream of things that were."

"How can I bear it, how can I live without him?" she asked despairingly.

Spiros was greeting her delightedly.

"Good-morning, Lady – very nice day for ride to Itea."

She forced a smile to her lips.

"I have not yet said good-bye to Nonika," she said to Dimitrios Argeros.

"I'll call her," he said and he turned and went into the Taverna.

As he went Athena heard a footstep behind her.

She turned thinking that Nonika must have approached from another direction, but coming round the side of the Taverna through some bushes where he must have been hiding was Kazandis!

For a moment she could not credit that it was really the Bandit and that he was actually walking towards her.

She felt her heart give a terrified jerk within her breast.

Without speaking, without saying anything, he came nearer still and before she had time to move away or obey her impulse to run he picked her up in his arms and flung her over his shoulder.

The shock of the impact on the hardness of his body took

her breath away. Then as she heard Spiros shout she managed to scream.

She screamed and screamed again and it was to Orion she called, her screams gradually giving way to his name which seemed stifled and ineffectual as she lay head downwards over Kazandis's shoulder.

He turned back through the bushes the way he had come, and moving at what seemed to Athena to be a tremendous speed, he started to climb the mountain behind the Taverna.

She tried to strike at him with her arms, but hanging down his back she was quite ineffectual and he held her tightly below the knees so that it was very difficult to struggle in any way at all.

He was climbing, climbing, and she tried to see if anyone was following them. But it was impossible for her to raise her head with the blood flowing into it.

Stones fell, dislodged by his feet, bouncing and rumbling their way down the steep mountainside, and as he zigzagged she knew that he was keeping to the goat-paths and also that he knew the way without faltering.

By now she was breathless and unable to scream any more or to cry out for Orion. She could only fear that in fact he had gone too far and not heard Spiros call or her own screams.

If he had not heard, she wondered if Spiros would ride after him and tell him what had occurred.

There was so much discomfort in hanging head downwards over Kazandis's back with the fur of his sheepskin coat tickling her face and smelling most unpleasant, that it was difficult to think clearly.

As they went higher there seemed to be a strange and uncanny silence around them. Athena wished to struggle again but she was too afraid.

She could see even with limited vision that the mountainside was very steep. There were patches of moss and occasionally twisting tree-trunks and small trees, their green leaves a strange contrast to the bare rocks.

She was well aware that where they were going was almost as steep and perilous as the Shining Cliffs, and should she fall she would roll down the mountainside in a manner which if it did not kill her would certainly bruise and maim her whole body.

'What can I do ... what can I do?' Athena thought frantically.

She knew that she was in Kazandis's power and supposed it would be impossible now for Orion to save her.

She thought that she must die before he touched her and wondered if it would be possible for her to shoot herself with his pistol or stab herself with his knife.

What was happening was so terrifying that her brain seemed to be paralysed by the horror of it.

The position in which he carried her made her feel almost apoplectic, and yet she knew that her only salvation lay in Orion.

She felt her whole being calling to him as she had managed to cry out at first, if only briefly.

Surely he would understand? Perhaps he would get a gun from somewhere in the village. Perhaps he would bring soldiers to her assistance.

But then she knew that even if he did so it would be too late.

What Kazandis intended to do to her would be done long before the Military could climb the cliff or Orion come to her assistance.

"I must ... die. God ... help me. I have to ... die!"

She felt that the God to whom she had prayed in the quietness and security of England was very far away, and she thought that now only Apollo or perhaps Hermes, the god of Travellers, could help her.

Higher and higher Kazandis climbed and now the stones beneath each foot-fall had become a kind of shower, and yet still he twisted and turned, obviously sure of his way between the craggy rocks.

Vaguely Athena realised that he was moving all the time

to the left but there was a whole range of the Parnassus mountains to choose from and it was impossible to speculate which way he was likely to go or where he was taking her.

Now it seemed to her that she had sudden glimpses of what seemed to be a sheer precipice beneath them, and because beside the horror of what was happening, it was terrifying to think of rolling down it, she shut her eyes.

Kazandis must have been carrying her for nearly half an hour, and Athena with the blood in her head found it impossible to think any longer, but only to feel choked and dizzy.

Suddenly he took a step upwards, bent his head then set her down roughly on the ground.

For a moment everything seemed to go black and she thought that she was dying.

Then as Athena opened her eyes she realised she was in a cave.

It was not a large cave and the roof under which she was lying only just enabled Kazandis to stand upright.

He was looking down at her and, dazed and bewildered though she was, the look in his eyes instinctively made her try to shrink away from him while her hands went to her breasts.

"Kazandis does not give up easily," he said in the boastful tones he had used in the Taverna the night before. "I want you and now you're mine!"

Athena could not speak, she could only stare up at him in terror.

"Yes, mine!" he repeated with satisfaction. "Get your breath. No-one will find you here."

It was not so much a question of her getting her breath, but of him getting his.

Perhaps because he had been in prison for so long, the burden of carrying her up the mountain had taken its toll even on such a strong man.

There were beads of sweat running down his forehead and over his cheeks.

He pulled off his sheepskin coat and flung it down on the ground and she saw that his shirt was stained and his hairy arms were wet.

He walked further into the cave and as her eyes followed him apprehensively she saw that the cave opened out and was far larger than it had first appeared from where she was lying.

From the darkness of the shadows Kazandis produced a bottle and pulling out the cork he lifted it to his lips and drank noisily.

"Have some?"

He held the bottle out to her and when she shook her head he said:

"Please yourself! There's plenty if you change your mind."

Now taking a dirty rag from his pocket, which he doubtless thought of as a handkerchief, he wiped his forehead and his cheeks and rubbed his hands on it before he flung it to the floor of the cave.

"You're a pretty piece," he said, "although you've not much to say for yourself."

"Let ... me ... go," Athena managed to articulate. "If you ... want money ... I can ... give it to you ... I am ... rich."

"Rich – when you are staying in a Taverna?" he laughed.

"It may seem ... strange," Athena answered, "but I am in fact ... very rich ... if you will let me ... go to ... safety ... I will pay you ... well."

"And how shall I collect it?" Kazandis asked jeeringly, "or will you ask the Military to hand it to me?"

"I will see you have it ... and that no-one will ... molest you," Athena said earnestly. "That I ... promise."

He laughed and the noise of it seemed to echo and re-echo round the cave.

"I've got all the money I want for the moment," he said, "and when I want more – I shall take it! But now I want you!"

He wiped his lips as he spoke with the back of his hand, and Athena thinking it was preliminary to kissing her gave a little cry of terror.

The mere fact that she was frightened seemed to please Kazandis and he smiled.

Then as he stepped towards her and she thought despairingly she must somehow try to snatch his knife and kill herself, he glanced towards the opening of the cave.

As if a thought had suddenly struck him, he went to it and looked out.

As Athena watched him it seemed to her that something seemed to hold his attention and he did not move but remained looking down below them.

A faint hope stirred within her and, moving for the first time since he had thrust her down onto the sandy floor, she got to her knees and edged forward so that she too could look out through the opening.

She saw what had attracted Kazandis's attention.

They were high up over what appeared to be almost an impassable precipice of steep rock.

Far beneath, almost directly below them, a man was climbing, not zig-zagging as they had done, but climbing directly upwards.

With an indescribable feeling of relief and gratitude Athena knew it was Orion.

Chapter Five

Kazandis stood staring down for some moments, then gave a grunt like an animal.

"You had better let me go," Athena said. "If people are coming to rescue me, you will not get the money I have offered you."

She thought for a moment that the Bandit was considering what she said. Then he laughed the same loud, jeering laugh which once again echoed round the cave.

"You think they'll find me?" he asked. "They'll never find me here, and I've caves, many caves which only the wolves know."

He came back into the cave and because she felt giddy looking down from such a great height, Athena also moved backwards.

He looked at her and his eyes narrowed unpleasantly and he moved as if he would touch her.

She gave a scream and before he could stop her she moved back again to the entrance of the cave and leaned out of it shouting:

"Orion! Orion! I am here! Save me!"

Her voice seemed to be swept away from her by the height and she felt it was shrill and ineffective; but it obviously disturbed Kazandis, for he seized her roughly and pulling her back into the cave threw her down on the floor.

"You be quiet!" he commanded.

There was something ferocious in the way he spoke, and although Athena tried to be brave she winced away from him in a manner which told him all too clearly how fearful she was.

"If you betray me you suffer for it!"

He raised his arm menacingly and for a second she thought he was going to strike her. Then as if another idea came to him he grunted again and moved further into the cave, disappearing into the shadows.

She wondered where he had gone.

Then because she could not believe that he was speaking the truth when he said it would be impossible for Orion to find her, she went once again to the opening and looked down.

For a moment she could not see him and she felt an icy hand clutching at her heart in case he had fallen or given up the climb as impossible.

Then she saw he was rounding a rock and perhaps following the track that Kazandis had taken.

She was staring down at him wondering whether she should scream to him again and risk Kazandis's anger, when she heard the Bandit coming back from the darkness.

She moved away, ashamed that she should be so afraid, unable to prevent an instinctive sense of self-protection.

Then she saw he was not looking at her, but instead was carrying in his hand a long-barrelled gun.

She looked at it with horror, until as he started to load it she asked in a quivering voice:

"Wh.. what are you ... going to ... do?"

"Kill the dog that's following me!" he answered.

She gave a cry.

"B.. but you ... cannot do that!"

"Who'll stop me?"

He tipped the powder into the breech and said as if he spoke to himself:

"Still dry after all this time. There's no better gun in the whole of Parnassus!"

With an effort Athena forced herself to speak quietly.

"I have told you that I am rich," she said. "Very rich. I will give you a thousand pounds ... five thousand pounds ...

ten thousand pounds, if you do not fire at that man who is following us."

Kazandis did not answer and after a moment Athena said:

"Perhaps you do not understand pounds. I will give you drachmas, a million if you like. You will be a rich man ... a very rich man. You can buy anything you like ... go anywhere you want."

She thought for a moment that he might be tempted by her offer. But then he looked up at her and she saw the sneer on his face as he said:

"Give it to me now and you can go!"

"Of course I cannot give it to you now," Athena replied. "I have not so much money here with me. But as I have told you I am rich, a very rich Englishwoman."

"I'm no fool," Kazandis said slowly. "Rich English tourists don't travel alone. They have friends with them, Guides, Couriers. They hire many donkeys and horses and have much luggage."

"All the things I own are in Mikis," Athena said, "and I have money there, a lot of money."

"With many people to guard it?"

There was no doubt that he did not believe her and thought she was lying.

Athena watched him white-faced as he finished loading the gun, then went to the mouth of the cave.

He crouched on the edge of it looking down and she knew that he was waiting until Orion presented him with a good target.

"You cannot do this ... you cannot!" she said frantically. "Listen to me ... please listen! I will give you all the money I promised you and I will be to you anything you want if you will spare the man down there. I will be your woman ... your wife ... whatever you require ... but please do not kill him!"

"I have you here with me," Kazandis answered. "I've all

the money I need. Why should I bargain?"

"Because I can give you so much more," Athena said frantically. "You must believe me. You must listen to what I tell you. A million drachmas shall be yours and I will stay with you and not go away, so long as you will spare the life of that man who you say will not be able to find us and is therefore doing you no harm."

Kazandis laughed. It was not a pleasant sound.

"I kill many men. Why should I spare this one?"

He put his gun to his shoulder as he spoke and looked down the barrel.

"Spare him ... please spare him!" Athena pleaded. "What can I say ... what can I offer you to make you understand that you must ... not do this ... terrible thing?"

She drew in her breath before she went on, her voice low and intense:

"It will be murder ... sheer murder and all the soldiers will be determined that you shall be found. They will find you wherever you may hide, and this time they will hang you ... there will be no escape."

"They'll not find me," Kazandis said confidently.

"They will! They will!" Athena cried.

Once again he was looking down the barrel, and now, although Athena could not see Orion, she realised that he must be below them but a little to the left.

Kazandis shifted his position so that the gun was pointing almost directly downwards.

He was taking aim, his finger was on the trigger.

"No! No!" Athena cried desperately.

Then as she thought he must fire and Orion would die she flung herself against him in an effort to snatch the gun from his hands.

She took him by surprise and although she was not strong the fact that she snatched at the gun made him lose his hold on it and it slipped from his hands.

He reached out towards it, grasping in the air to catch it before it slipped from his reach. As he did so, hardly realising what she was doing, Athena pushed his shoulder with all her strength.

For a moment it seemed as if she made no impact upon him, then Kazandis strove to keep his balance and fell.

He gave one last grunt and with a cry which was like that of an animal in agony he disappeared from sight.

One moment he was there, a monstrous figure in the opening of the cave, and the next minute he was gone and all she could see was the sky and the sun was blinding her eyes.

Athena had also lost her balance in her effort against Kazandis, and she lay sprawled on the sandy floor, too bemused, too shocked by what had happened to move.

Then suddenly the horror of it swept over her.

She had killed a man!

Killed him intentionally and deliberately ... although it had all happened so quickly that it was hard to know the exact moment when she had meant it to happen.

She lay panting. Then because she could not bear to look below and see the broken remains of the man she had killed, she moved back into the cave and sat with her back against the wall and covered her face with her hands.

It seemed as if she had passed through a nightmare from which now she could not wake.

It seemed altogether unreal: her discomfort and fear while being carried up the mountain; the terror she felt at Kazandis's presence; the agony she had suffered knowing he intended to kill Orion!

Now he was dead – and she was responsible.

She sat trembling, trying to think clearly, but all she was conscious of was the violent beating of her heart and a kind of indescribable horror that prevented her thinking of anything but Kazandis's scream as he fell.

Then suddenly there was a sound and without taking her hands from her face she knew that someone had entered the cave.

For a moment it was impossible to move or to breathe;

then Orion's arms were around her and he was holding her close to him.

"It is all right, my darling," he said. "It is over. You are safe."

"I ... killed him! Oh, Orion ... I killed ... him!"

He held her a little closer and after a moment she said:

"He meant ... to shoot you ... and nothing I could ... say ... nothing I could ... offer him would ... stop him."

"He is dead," Orion said quietly. "That is all that matters. He did not hurt you, my precious little goddess?"

"N..no," Athena whispered.

"Put your hands down and listen to me."

Athena felt so weak that she was prepared to do anything she was told.

She lowered her hands and raised her eyes.

He was very near her and now that she could look at him the feeling of horror began to recede.

"I know what you have been through," Orion said in a low voice, "but darling, you are to forget it ever happened, and you are to tell no-one – no-one, do you understand? – that it was due to you that Kazandis died."

"B..but I k..killed him."

"To save me," he said, "and it was very brave and very wonderful of you. But I would not wish you to be interrogated, because that is what it would mean, by the Military. And I do not want you in the future to be pointed out as the woman who killed Kazandis."

"Was it very ... wrong and very ... wicked of me?" Athena asked.

He smiled and it seemed to illuminate his face.

"My darling, it is what hundreds of people have been trying to do for a very long time. He was an animal, a reptile, an enemy of the people, a man without morals, without principles and without mercy. The world is well rid of him."

Athena gave a little sigh and laid her head against Orion's shoulder.

"Remember, my sweet, that he over-balanced and fell — that is what happened."

He drew her close, as he went on:

"How could I imagine that such a terrible thing would happen to you the moment I left your side?"

"He was ... hiding in the bushes by the Taverna," Athena said. "When he carried me ... away I was only afraid you would not ... hear me calling for ... you.'"

"I heard Spiros and I heard you scream," Orion replied. "I could not imagine what had occurred."

"But you ... came back."

"Of course I came back," he answered. "I knew that you of all people would not scream unless something very terrible had occurred."

Athena gave a little sigh.

"What did you ... feel when you ... knew what had ... happened?"

For a moment Orion did not reply, and because she was surprised she looked up at him.

His eyes were on hers and after a moment he said:

"I knew that not only must I rescue you, but also that I must never lose you again."

Athena looked at him wide-eyed, then he said:

"You belong to me, my darling. I knew it when we first met, and when we kissed in the moonlight and together touched the summit of bliss."

Athena made a little movement as if she would draw nearer to him, but she did not speak and after a moment he went on:

"I thought I was doing the right thing for both of us when I decided that we must go our separate ways, and we would remember as if it were a dream what we had meant to each other."

"And now ... ?"

"Now I know that I cannot live without you. You are mine, Athena, and nothing and nobody shall ever keep us apart."

Athena felt as though the whole cave was illuminated with a brilliant light.

There was a tremor in her voice as she asked:

"Do you ... mean that? Are you ... sure of what you are ... saying?"

"Quite, quite sure," he answered. "I love you, my darling and I know that you love me."

His voice seemed to ring out as he went on:

"It is not just a question of love, it is because your spirit is my spirit, as my soul is your soul. We belong to one another. We are one and I will spend the whole of my life protecting you and taking care of you."

"That is all I ... want," Athena whispered. "I love ... you! I have loved you from the very first moment I met you and although it has been ... wonderful it has also been ... agonising."

Her voice broke on the words.

"My precious, my poor little love. You shall not suffer any more," he said with a deep tenderness in his voice.

Then his lips found hers and she knew she surrendered her whole self, body and soul, to his kiss.

* * *

Later when they had told each other of their love, and kissed again and again, Orion smoothed back Athena's hair from her flushed cheeks and said:

"Now, my darling, I think we should make plans to return to civilisation. It is still quite early in the day, but there is a lot to do if we are to be married this evening."

"M .. married?"

Athena gazed at him wide-eyed.

"I thought that was what we were talking about," he said with a smile, "but of course I have not really asked you. Will you marry me, my lovely one?"

He saw the expression in her eyes, then he put his hand under her chin and tipped her face up to his.

"I know," he said. "I know all the things we ought to say – 'we do not know each other very well' – but we do! 'We have only just met' – but that is not true! We have known each other since the beginning of time! 'We ought to have a conventional ceremony with all our relatives present' – but do either of us want that?"

"No ... no," Athena said instinctively.

"That is exactly what I feel," he said, "and because I dare not let you out of my sight – because I have no intention of losing you – I intend to marry you this evening. Nothing else is of any consequence."

"Oh, Orion ... do you really ... mean it?" Athena asked.

"You have not answered my question," he said with a smile. "Will you marry me?"

Just for a moment Athena thought of her family, of her Aunt waiting for her in the Palace, of her grandmother, of the King in Athens. Then she knew that Orion was right, and that none of them mattered.

"I want to marry you," she said, "more than I have ever wanted anything in my whole life."

"Then let us get married," Orion smiled.

"I wondered when you were ... leaving me whether in fact you had a ... wife already."

He laughed.

"You need have no fears on that score, and I am not going to ask if you have a husband. No-one could be so soft and sweet, so innocent, and not be as pure as Athena herself."

Because there was a note in his voice that made her feel shy, Athena hid her face against his neck.

He kissed her hair, then said:

"There are a thousand things we have to tell each other which will give us something to talk about on our honeymoon! But all that concerns me at this moment is that you should be my wife and that no-one – and I mean no-one – shall take you from me."

She supposed he was thinking of Kazandis, but her thoughts went to the Prince.

Supposing by marrying her Orion should incur the hostility of the Prince he had supplanted?

Then she remembered how rich she was and knew that if the Prince resented their marriage and made trouble for them in Greece they could go elsewhere.

The whole world was theirs, and she need not be afraid.

"But in order to get married," Orion was saying, "we have to get away from this eagle's nest."

He went to the mouth of the cave as he spoke and stood looking down.

After a moment Athena followed him.

She took one glance at the precipice beneath them; then afraid that she might see Kazandis's body lying somewhere at the foot of it she looked away and said:

"I am ... afraid of ... heights."

"I thought perhaps you might be," he answered, "and this is no ordinary height. Kazandis hid himself very cleverly, but fortunately I guessed where he had gone."

"How could you have guessed?" Athena asked.

"After he was captured two years ago, a survey of the mountains showed the most likely spots in which he had his hiding-places. There are a large number of caves of all sorts in this part of the world, and when I saw him carrying you up the mountain I knew the whereabouts of this particular cave and was sure that was where he was taking you."

"It was lucky ... very lucky that you should have ... known that," Athena exclaimed.

She could not help remembering the expression on Kazandis's face as he looked at her and the lust she had seen in his eyes.

As if he knew what she was thinking, Orion put his arms around her and kissed first her eyes, then her cheeks, and lastly her mouth.

"You are to think of no-one but me," he said masterfully. "I am jealous even of Kazandis if he occupies your thoughts."

"I want ... only to ... think of ... you," Athena murmured.

He kissed her again, then he went to the entrance of the cave and gave a shout of joy.

"Here they come!" he said. "I thought Dimitrios Argeros would not fail me."

"What is it? Who is there?" Athena asked.

"I shouted to him as I started to climb after you for some of the men from the village to bring ropes with them," Orion answered. "I was sure there must be an easier way than climbing directly up the mountainside, but I could not wait to take it myself."

Athena knew with a little throb of her heart why he had realised only too well that there was every reason for haste.

He was aware why Kazandis had carried her away, and if he had not arrived until now it would have been too late.

"Could any man be more wonderful?" she asked herself.

* * *

Athena thought only of Orion all the time he and the men from the village were helping her down the mountainside.

It was not easy although she was roped to Orion and he to several others.

There were moments when the world below seemed to swim before her eyes, and she thought that however tightly they held her she must fall as Kazandis had fallen to die on the rocks below.

Somehow, although they took a long time, they managed it and when finally they came down into the village Madame Argeros was waiting to fold Athena in her arms and kiss her as if she was her own long-lost child.

It was difficult to say anything amid the babble of noise, the congratulations that were showered upon Orion, and the excited comments of everyone, including the children.

Madame Argeros took Athena into the Taverna and made her sit down on a chair.

"You must be exhausted," she said. "There's some coffee waiting for you and that will do you more good than the wine which Orion will be opening as soon as he can get here."

"I would ... rather have coffee," Athena managed to say.

"Drink it up," Madame admonished, "then you are going straight upstairs to lie down on the bed. I will bring you up something to eat."

Because Athena really did feel exhausted she drank her coffee as Madame had ordered, and went upstairs.

"You will be more comfortable in the big bed," Madame Argeros said. "Nonika has put fresh sheets on it."

Athena was only too glad to agree.

She knew it was stupid of her but she felt an aversion to the other room where she had been so frightened when Kazandis let himself down from the roof in search of her.

Madame Argeros helped her out of her gown. Then, slipping on her night-dress which had been left behind in her bag on the horse, Athena lay back against the pillows with a little sigh.

"I'll cook something light and appetising," Madame Argeros said, "and Nonika shall bring it up."

"Thank you, Madame. You are very kind."

"We are ashamed and humiliated that such things should happen to a lady like you when you have been our guest," Madame Argeros said, "but now that evil man is dead there will be no more troubles."

"Are there no other bandits?" Athena asked.

"Plenty of them," Madame replied, "but they are not like him. Most bandits are only beggars, who are hungry and want to eat. They're poor and they ask for a little money! But Kazandis was different, he was a murderer!"

She went from the room as she spoke and Athena shivered.

Kazandis might be a murderer, but she had murdered him! Then she told herself she must not think about it, but only of Orion, as he had told her to do.

She was to be married to Orion!

Somehow she could hardly believe it was true that she was to be his wife as she longed to be; there would be no problems about the Prince to be solved, no question of whether she should return to England or not.

The astonishment and inevitable reproaches of her relatives did not concern her.

For the moment she would only have to cope with Aunt Beatrice, but later she would have to tell her father what had happened and of course her grandmother.

It was the Dowager Marchioness who would mind most and feel that Athena had betrayed her trust.

"They will love Orion when they meet him," Athena told herself confidently.

But any such meeting was a long way off and for the moment there was only one thing to worry about, and that was the attitude the Prince might take.

Athena did not know anything about Greek law, but she expected that the Nobility and certainly minor Royalties in every country were important and powerful and to offend one of them could result in penalties which were not only social ones.

Then she told herself again that if things became difficult she and Orion would leave Greece.

In which case, she thought uneasily, they would have to live on her money.

Here was another difficulty she had not faced before.

She knew nothing about Orion, and yet instinctively she was aware that he was proud.

She was sure he was a man who would think it beneath him to accept money from a woman: a man must always be the master in his own house and that included his wife.

"I shall have to tell him who I am," Athena thought, but she felt afraid.

He loved her enough to marry her whoever she might be, but she supposed that he thought of her as a quite ordinary Englishwoman from an ordinary family, with perhaps a little money of her own, enough at any rate to travel round the world.

But that was very different from marrying a great heiress and a woman who had come to Greece to marry one of the reigning Princes.

"If I tell him he might not ... marry me," Athena thought.

She felt herself trembling and knew here was something she must avoid at all costs.

He had told her nothing about himself, he had asked no questions where she was concerned; but the moment would come eventually when they must be frank with each other.

Then if she was not already his wife Orion might refuse to go through with the marriage which he himself had suggested.

She knew as she thought of it that she could not – she dare not – lose him for the second time.

It had been a pain and an agony unlike anything she had ever known in the whole of her quiet life when she had watched him ride away from her on the black stallion and knew that he was riding out of her life forever.

And because her suffering had been so intense she had hardly had time to realise that it was tearing her into pieces when Kazandis appeared and carried her away.

Now she knew that what she had suffered was like dying a thousand deaths and she could not go through that again.

"I will not ... tell him," she decided. "I will tell him ... nothing until we are married. Nothing ... nothing!"

In her mind she said the words defiantly as if she challenged the fates themselves to wrench her happiness from her at the eleventh hour.

As if in answer she heard at that moment Orion's feet coming up the stairs.

He knocked at the door of her room but it was open and even as he knocked he could see her lying in what had been his bed.

He came towards her and she thought she had never seen a man look so happy.

"Madame Argeros told me you were resting, my darling," he said, "but I had to see you."

Athena stretched out her hands towards him.

"I wanted to see you."

"You are all right? You do not feel ill?"

She shook her head.

"Only a little tired."

"That is not surprising," he said, "and I want you to rest. I will arrange for our wedding to take place in the cool of the evening, but I am afraid that the whole village will wish to celebrate afterwards – do you mind?"

"I mind nothing as long as I can be your wife."

He took her hand in his and kissed her fingers one after another, then pressed his lips into the softness of her palm.

"I can hardly believe that everything that happened this morning really took place," he said. "But now you are safe – and you belong to me!"

She felt herself thrill at his tone of voice.

But when instinctively she lifted her face towards his, her lips ready for his kiss, he looked down at her and said:

"You are not to tempt me, Athena. I want you to rest, but if I start kissing you now it will be very difficult for me to stop or to leave you alone as I intend to do."

"You will not go ... far?"

There was a touch of fear in her voice.

"Only to the Church, because I have to speak with the Priest," he said. "Do you mind, my darling, being married in the Greek Orthodox religion to which I belong?"

"I do not mind how we are married ... as long as we ... are," Athena answered.

"I really feel we should be married in the Temple of Apollo," Orion smiled, "but the Priests are long dead, and I am determined to tie you to me by every vow and nuptial bond that exists so that you can never escape."

"I would never want to," Athena murmured.

They looked into each other's eyes and she knew that Orion drew in his breath.

It was almost impossible, Athena thought, to be closer to one another than they were at this moment in their love for each other.

Then with an effort Orion kissed her hand again.

"I am going now, my darling. There was really only one thing I came to ask you and it seems extraordinary after all that has happened that I do not know your name."

Athena had anticipated this question. A lot had been written about her in the newspapers in Athens when she arrived with her Aunt and she was afraid that if she told him her real name Orion might connect it with the English heiress who was visiting Greece and had been received by the King.

Yet when she first thought of it she asked herself whether if she was married by any other name it would be legal.

Then she remembered, almost as if fate had provided for such an emergency, what she had been told had happened at her christening.

Her American Godmother, Mrs. Mayville, who had later left her the huge fortune, had been asked to hold the baby in her arms. She had been instructed that when the Parson said: "Name this child," she should reply: "Mary Emmeline Athena".

But Athena's Godmother was not only delighted with her Godchild, but also wished to give her something of herself.

She must have thought over what she intended to do while the Service began and the baby lay sleeping peacefully in her arms wrapped in the long lace-edged robe in which every member of the Wade family had been christened for centuries.

Finally when the Godparents had promised to "renounce the devil and all his works" and sanctified the water in the font he turned to Mrs. Mayville. She handed him the baby, and he said:

"Name this child."

"Mary Emmeline Athena Mayville," she answered.

There was a little gasp from the Marquess and the other relatives, but before they could think what to do the Parson had intoned solemnly:

"Mary Emmeline Athena Mayville I baptise thee In the Name of the Father, of the Son and of the Holy Ghost. Amen."

Athena's head had received the Holy Water and for the first time she cried, "Letting the devil out of her!" as her Nanny said later with satisfaction.

Afterwards the Marquess had stormed in a fury about it.

"I told you the Wades have never been given fancy names! Athena Mayville! Have you ever heard of such a combination?"

"I am sorry, dearest," Athena's mother replied. "I had no idea that my friend intended anything quite so unexpected. But there was nothing we could do."

"I should have stopped the ceremony," the Marquess said. "It is outrageous that my daughter should be saddled for life with such names!"

"Perhaps we could just forget them," the Marchioness said soothingly. "After all, we shall always call her Mary and there is no reason for her ever to use any other name."

The Marquess was gradually reassured, but Athena learnt as she grew older that her Godmother was in disgrace and was seldom invited back to Wadebridge Castle.

However, when she died and left all her money to Athena, the Marquess's antagonism was noticeably modified and he no longer flew into a rage if she was mentioned in his presence.

Now Athena thought her Godmother had done her a good turn.

Her name indeed was Athena Mayville legally, and she was quite certain that once married it would be impossible for the ceremony to be annulled because she had not used all her other names.

Orion was waiting for her answer and she smiled up at him.

"Athena Mayville," she said. "And now it is only fair that you should tell me yours."

"It is very Greek," he answered. "Theodoros."

"I like it," she said. "I shall be very proud to be Athena Theodoros."

She spoke with such sincerity in her voice that Orion could not prevent himself from kissing her.

It was a hard, quick kiss but, as if he no longer trusted himself, he rose to his feet and walked towards the door.

"Sleep now, my darling," he said. "There is nothing to make you afraid. I shall rest later in the next room, and if you want me you have only to call."

"I shall remember ... that," Athena answered.

As it happened she fell asleep almost as soon as he had left her and she did not hear Nonika bring her food or take it away again.

She slept and slept, dreaming happily of Orion and not even in her dreams did the shadow of Kazandis disturb her.

She awoke drowsily to find Nonika was coming into her room carrying a can of hot water.

"I thought you would want to wash," she said in her shy manner as Athena opened her eyes, "and I've brought you some coffee. Mama is cooking you an omelette."

"Thank you."

"And I have sponged your gown and pressed it," Nonika went on, "but I am afraid it does not look very nice."

Athena sat up in bed.

She was to be married and for the first time she realised that she had nothing to wear.

She could hardly bear to think that on what was the most important day in her life she had only the gown that she had worn yesterday, and which she knew had been in a terrible state by the time they had brought her down the mountainside.

The ropes had marked the waist, and the bushes, some of them with thorny claws, had clutched at her skirts as she passed them.

The dust and dirt from the bare rocks had done the rest.

Nonika laid it over a chair, but even though the full skirt was uncreased it was still badly marked.

"Oh, Nonika!" Athena exclaimed. "How can I be married in that?"

It was woman calling to woman, a cry for help that was very feminine.

Nonika was silent for a moment, then she said:

"I have a suggestion, but I would not like you to think it impertinent."

"I would not think anything you suggested impertinent," Athena said, "especially if it was helpful."

She rose from the bed as she spoke and walked across the room in her bare feet to look at the gown.

"I do want to look beautiful for Orion," she said almost beneath her breath.

"I understand," Nonika said, "I would feel the same. I have a gown that I could lend you, but you might not like it."

"Could I see it?" Athena asked.

She saw the smile in Nonika's eyes before she ran from the room, then Athena wondered what she could possibly provide that would not make her look even more shabby than she would appear in her own soiled gown.

She thought of all the beautiful dresses she had brought to Greece in her trousseau and longed for Orion to see her in them.

It was easy, Athena thought, to say that clothes did not matter beside one's feelings, but there was no woman in the whole world who did not wish to look beautiful and at her best on her wedding-day.

She almost felt as if she would rather postpone the wedding than be married looking drab and bedraggled, as was inevitable unless Nonika could provide her with something different.

But what could the daughter of a Taverna-keeper have to offer?

Athena did not ask the question disparagingly but practically.

All the gowns she had brought with her to Greece had been from the most expensive dressmakers in London.

If she had not been conscious that she must be extremely smart and impressive when married to the Prince of Parnassus, her grandmother had certainly been determined that she should outshine every member of the fashionable Athenian Society.

"The Queen is noted for her elegance," the Dowager Marchioness had said, "and when there are women in Athens like Lady Ellenborough you cannot afford to be anything but very smart."

It was the first time that Athena had heard of Lady Ellenborough, but there were plenty of people to tell her of the English Beauty's adventures and her flamboyant behaviour with one lover after another.

The stories of Lady Ellenborough, or the Countess Theotoky as she was now, lost nothing in the telling. She was called "The Queen of Love and Beauty", and her loveliness was framed by exquisite clothes.

"Perhaps Orion knows women like that," Athena thought now. "How can I marry him looking little better than a beggar-maid?"

It did not help to recall that she was very much the opposite, which was something she was still afraid to tell her future husband.

It only made her feel sadly that some of the happiness and glamour of her wedding was being taken from her simply because she did not look as a bride should.

She walked to the small mirror which stood on the chest-of-drawers and stared at her reflection.

Orion thought her beautiful – she knew that – but because she wanted him to go on thinking so for the rest of his life she could imagine nothing more depressing than for him to start off their wedded life together by feeling sorry for her.

And that undoubtedly was how he would feel when he saw her in her old gown.

Almost despairingly Athena waited as she heard Nonika coming back up the stairs.

Had she a solution? Was there anything she could offer as an alternative to her own clothes?

Nonika entered the room, and Athena drew in her breath.

In her arms she carried almost reverently a gown which Athena knew instinctively was to be Nonika's own wedding-dress and she recognised it as a native costume of Parnassus.

It was very elaborate and beautiful.

The gown was white, made simply with open sleeves, the soft material edged both at the hem and on the sleeves with the most intricate and exquisite coral and gold embroidery.

The same colours richly embroidered with gold formed an apron and the front of the bodice was embellished in the same way.

To be worn round the neck was a huge necklace of wrought gold fringed with coins, set with five rows of turquoises and corals of varying sizes encircled with what appeared to be small diamonds.

Athena gasped and Nonika explained:

"The necklace has been in our family for many, many years, all Greek families have them."

She paused to add sadly:

"Or they did have them, many have had to be sold for food or to pay the terrible taxes."

"It is perfectly lovely," Athena exclaimed.

"The dress was made by me and my mother," Nonika continued. "We embroidered all through the winter, and now at last it is finished!"

"But you cannot wish anyone else to wear it!" Athena protested.

"You will look very beautiful in it," Nonika replied. "A Greek bride for Orion."

"Will you really lend it to me?"

"I should be honoured."

"It is kind ... so very kind of you," Athena answered, "but you must show me how to wear it, how to put it on."

"I will show you," Nonika agreed. "It is not difficult."

When she had been staying in Athens Athena had seen many Greek girls wearing their native costume and thought how attractive they looked.

But Nonika's gown was not only lovelier than those she had seen, it was also particularly becoming to her.

There was a white veil with which she covered her hair and perched on the top of it was a little gold cap, also embellished with turquoises and coral and with a row of gold coins which outlined her forehead.

When she looked at herself in the mirror she thought she looked quite different from the way she had looked before and yet it seemed a more fitting frame for her oval face and huge grey eyes than anything else she had ever worn.

"You look lovely! Lovely!" Nonika exclaimed. "And now we will show you to Orion."

Athena took a last look at herself in the mirror.

Would he think her beautiful, she wondered, or would he perhaps think what she wore was too like fancy-dress?

Then she told herself that this was after all, the type of costume which all Greek girls wore and as Nonika had said she was to be a Greek bride.

Nonika ran ahead of her down the stairs to say she was coming and as Athena moved a little shyly into the kitchen Orion rose from the table at which he had been sitting.

She only needed one glance at his eyes, one look at his face to know exactly what he thought.

There was no need for words.

To him she was as beautiful as he had expected her to be.

Chapter Six

The men were dancing the *zeimbekiko* with a verve and a vigour that was exciting for those who watched them.

Athena thought it would be impossible for a single other guest, however thin, to squeeze into the kitchen of the Taverna.

They were certainly a colourful throng to look at, all wearing what she realised were their best and most treasured costumes, the women brilliant in red and blue, yellow and magenta.

Those who could not get inside the Taverna were sitting outside on the verandah or leaning through the open windows into the room.

It was hot, it was noisy, and yet at the same time it had a spontaneous gaiety that she had never encountered before.

The whole village had turned out for their wedding.

When she had come out from the Taverna with Orion she found that they had already congregated outside around the ancient, open carriage that was to carry them to the Church.

The horse which drew it was decorated with flowers, even the hubs of the wheels had bows of ribbon on them, and the closed hood was piled with hibiscus, bougainvillaea and blossoms from other shrubs.

A cheer went up as Athena and Orion appeared, and as he helped her into the carriage she realised that if she had borrowed her wedding-gown he also must have borrowed the clothes he wore.

He was wearing the full-sleeved traditional white shirt and over it a gold edged bolero which was exquisitely embroidered with flowers in all colours of the rainbow.

There was a red silk handkerchief around his neck and a red cummerbund around his waist, but instead of the stiff-pleated, white-skirted *fustanella* that many of the other men wore he had on tight-fitting black trousers which were extremely becoming.

He did in fact look so handsome and attractive that Athena felt her heart turn over with happiness.

As the horse started off he took her hand in his.

"All these people love you," she said as the crowd cheered and followed the carriage, the children running beside it excitedly down the narrow road towards the village.

"As everyone you meet in my country will love you, my darling," he answered.

She looked into his eyes and found it hard to remember anything except that she was to be his wife and that already she belonged to him in everything but name.

It was only a short distance to the Church which was small and built Byzantine fashion in the shape of a cross.

As Athena walked into it on Orion's arm and found the Priest waiting for them, she realised it would have been quite impossible for even a tenth of the people following them to get inside the small building.

But she soon realised that Orion had thought of this and everything was arranged.

Only the Argeros family followed them into the Church, while the rest stood outside the open door in respectful silence.

Although Athena had seen the Priests of the Greek Orthodox religion walking about the streets with their black beards and flowing black robes, she had not before seen one of the brilliantly coloured vestments such as was worn by the Priest who was waiting to marry them.

Of shimmering silver and gold the embroidery seemed to be part of the flowers outside, and the fragrance in the building itself reminded her of the grasses around the shrine of Apollo.

Innumerable candles and the seven silver sanctuary lamps glittered on the mosaics and gold carvings with which the Church was decorated, and they also illuminated the dozens of sacred Icons which hung on every available wall.

Athena had been afraid that she would not understand the ceremony, but as soon as it started she realised that the Priest was conducting the Service in Katharevousa, which was the Greek she knew.

She and Orion made their vows and when they knelt in front of the Priest, Dimitrios Argeros held over both their heads the linked wreaths which symbolised their union as man and wife.

Nonika, wearing a pretty gown, but very simple compared to the one she had lent to Athena, had held the bride's bouquet during the Service.

Orion had placed it in the carriage and it was a small posy fashioned of white irises. Athena knew that as they were the flowers of the gods it was for both of them a symbolic gift.

The service in the small Church was very beautiful, and as the fragrance of the flowers and the incense mingled together Athena felt that nothing could be more inspiring or more holy.

She dedicated herself for all time to Orion and felt that he did the same to her.

When he placed the ring on her finger she saw the expression on his face and knew that he was deeply moved. She thought that in marrying the man she loved and who loved her she was the most fortunate woman in the whole world.

Whatever difficulties lay ahead, whatever obstacles they might encounter, however many recriminations awaited them because of their action in getting married so quietly and secretly, it would always be the supreme moment in their lives.

Athena knew that nothing could be more fitting or indeed more wonderful than that she should marry Orion without a fashionable congregation, surrounded only by those who loved him for himself and had nothing to give or take except true friendship.

The Priest blessed them, then as they rose to their feet Orion put his arms around her and kissed her.

It was a kiss which was sacred and holy and she knew she would ask nothing more of God than that she should be his wife.

"My heart, my mind and my soul," he said very softly in English so that only she could hear.

As they turned to go out into the sunshine where their friends were waiting both of them radiated a happiness that was not of this world.

But the villagers of Delphi were not to be deprived of their fun.

Athena and Orion were driven back up the hill, but now the carriage was invaded and there were men and children hanging on to the sides and the back and flowers were thrown at them by the women until they sat knee-deep in blossom.

At the Taverna Madame Argeros had laid out a spread of food which made Athena gasp.

She could only guess that all the women of the village must have contributed, for it would have been impossible for any one person to cook so much in so short a time.

There were tables groaning under plentiful but not expensive food – for the villagers were poor – but the best each could contribute.

Bottles were opened, and Athena and Orion were toasted a hundred times as they sat together at the top of the table.

Athena was too excited to want to eat but Madame Argeros pressed the delicacies upon her and she did not wish to be disappointing.

When the food was finished and the tables taken away the dancing began and now Athena could see as she had wanted to ever since she came to Greece the folk dances.

These had evolved through the centuries containing in

each one of them the taste of the different nationalities, creeds and cultures which had been part of Greece at one time or another.

And Athena heard for the first time the real Greek music which was something she had not been able to listen to at the Court in Athens.

Now she saw the *aulos*, or reed pipe, which she knew was associated with the wine-god Dionysus. Beside the pipes, there was the flute and the lyre, and the *tympanon* which was a hand beaten frame drum and the *crotala*, hand-clappers, and the *cymbala*, which were cymbals.

As if as a concession to modernity there was also an accordion played by a young man wearing a *fustanella* and the Greek cap with the long black tassel that reached to his waist.

Those who were musical seemed to Athena to be more vividly and exotically dressed than the others.

The entertainment which had been put on for the bride and bridegroom started with the *chassapiko* which Orion told her was "the butchers' dance" originating from Constantinople and was danced by four men who hissed and snapped their fingers to a rhythm clearly marked by their foot-beats.

It was gay and amusing and was followed by the arrival of the *bouzoukia* which was a large awkward-looking mandolin which added to the other music nostalgic notes which sometimes seemed weighted with sorrow.

Each performance was greeted with cheers and prolonged applause and shouts of "Bravo!"

A quick and lively *serviko* which Athena thought was probably of Slav origin had everybody stamping their feet and swaying their shoulders.

She was certain that if there had been room everybody would have joined in.

Now, as the men performed the *zeimbekiko*, their arms reaching across each other's shoulders and having strangely enough a grace which she had not expected, she found herself wondering why in England dancing was considered to be only a feminine accomplishment.

There was no doubt that the Greek men enjoyed every moment of their rhythmic movements and they danced because they loved dancing.

It gave them a feeling of warmth and camaraderie towards those with whom they shared this pleasure.

The *zeimbekiko* evoked frenzied applause. Then with the soft throbbing of the *bouzoukia* a man began to sing the timeless strain of a lover's serenade.

It was a flowing melodic Ionian *cantade* which Athena knew had the power to ravish the ear and melt the heart of all those who listened to it.

Now everyone was silent, their dark eyes filled with emotion.

Because she too was moved by the singer's deep voice which had an unmistakable throb in it, Athena sought Orion's hand.

She felt his spontaneous reaction almost crush her fingers bloodless. Then as the singer finished and after a moment's pause of appreciation more congratulatory than any other expression, the noise broke out.

It was then that Orion pulled Athena to her feet and they slipped away into the back of the kitchen almost before anybody realised they had moved.

She thought he intended to take her upstairs, but instead he opened a door at the side of the building which she did not know existed and they stepped out into the star-strewn night.

There was a path leading through the bushes which led them to the road without having to pass through the crowds outside the Taverna.

Athena did not speak, she only let Orion lead her where he would and felt a rising excitement because at last they were alone together.

The road through the village now seemed empty and

deserted. They walked along it and gradually the music from the Taverna grew fainter and fainter.

It was almost like stepping into another world and Athena was aware of the quietness and the inexpressible serenity which was part of the Sanctuary.

The stars were vivid in the sky and the moon was rising.

She felt her pulses quicken at the thought that Orion was taking her to where they had known the wonder of their first kiss and she had given him her heart for all time.

But when they reached the narrow path that led up to the Temple of Apollo and beyond again to the Theatre, Orion kept on down the road.

Athena glanced at him enquiringly, but he did not speak and because there was no need for words between them she did not ask where they were going.

She knew instinctively that he was taking her to where he had found her, to the shrine of her namesake – the Temple of Athena.

Their footsteps made no sound on the dry, sandy road and Athena felt almost as if they floated past the ravine through which gushed the Castalian Cascade, until they came to the steps which led down to the shrine.

Now they had to pass through the closely growing olive trees until in the clearing they saw the three lovely Doric columns of the Tholos.

The moonlight was shining on their fluted marble so that they seemed to sparkle with almost a crystalline beauty.

Then as she looked at them wonderingly Orion's arms went round her and her thoughts were only of him.

"My wife!" he said softly as if he wished to convince himself that the words were true.

It was the first time he had spoken since they left the Taverna.

Holding her close he looked down at her face and the moonlight revealed to each of them the expressions in their eyes.

"You are more beautiful, my darling, than I believed it

possible for any woman to be!" he said. "And now you are mine – mine for eternity – because if we have been separated before, we cannot be separated again."

"I love ... you! Oh, Orion ... I love ... you!" Athena whispered.

"Love is such an inadequate word for what I feel for you," he answered. "Everything about you is perfect, not only your beauty, my precious one, but your sweetness, your kindness, and most of all your courage."

"I am not really ... brave," Athena replied. "Only when I think of ... you."

She raised her lips to his as she spoke, his mouth came down on hers and she felt as if a streak of fire ran through her, magical, ecstatic and with a radiance that was desire.

Orion held her close and still closer. Then with his lips still keeping her captive his hands removed the little gold embroidered cap on her head and the veil which covered her hair.

He drew out the pins which held it in place so that it fell over her shoulders as it had done when she had been lying in his bed.

Gently he unfastened the huge gold necklace and then she felt his fingers unbuttoning her wedding-gown.

It was difficult to think of anything but the wonder of his lips and the fact that the fire he had evoked in her seemed to run over her whole body, burning its way from the top of her head to the very points of her toes.

Athena felt her dress fall to the ground followed by the garments she wore beneath it.

She was not shy. She felt as if she was lifted by Orion's lips into a mystic rapture which swept away all human emotions and she was ethereal and spiritually one with the night.

Orion raised his head and looked at her.

"You are divine!" he said hoarsely. "The goddess at whose feet I worship!"

Just for a moment he stood not touching her, then he

pulled her into his arms and carried her beneath an ancient olive tree.

Athena felt the grass and flowers bending beneath her body and there was the fragrance of wild lilies and the scent of thyme.

She looked up and her eyes were dazzled by the brilliance of the moon-shafts shining through the branches. And she was conscious of a strange glitter in the air.

For a second she thought she had lost Orion, only to find him standing above her and he looked as she had seen him once before, his slim, athletic body silver in the moonlight.

She felt that he was haloed by the stars after which he was named and that he shimmered with them until she was looking at a constellation.

Then he was beside her, touching her so that she quivered and trembled because of the sensations he awakened and the fire in her breasts seemed to burst into a flame.

He moved and his heart beat against her heart and she could no longer think.

She only knew that he carried her up into the sky. She was conscious of a strange glitter in the air and there was the beat of silver wings as, glorious and omnipotent, they were gods.

* * *

Riding down the incline which led them South from the Sanctuary, Athena turned to smile at Orion who was still having a little difficulty in keeping his stallion under control.

It would be hard to explain to him, she thought, how during her journey up from Itea to Delphi she had longed to ride as she was riding now, free and untrammelled in the early morning sunshine.

But as if he understood without words what she was thinking he drew his horse alongside hers and said:

"Are you happy, my precious one?"

There was no need for Athena to answer him in words, her eyes met his and he thought he had never known a woman could look so radiant, so lovely.

They had left the Taverna very early, in fact Athena felt that she had hardly closed her eyes before Orion awakened her.

"We have a long ride ahead of us, my darling love," he said. "As I do not wish you to be exhausted by the heat I would like to start as soon as you are ready."

"Is... it morning?" Athena asked drowsily.

"Yes, darling, it is morning," he answered, "and the first day of our marriage."

She opened her eyes at that and lifted her arms towards him, but he took her hands and kissed them one after another before he said:

"If I kiss your lips my beautiful, adorable wife, I shall come back to bed and stay with you there for the rest of the day!"

Athena blushed and he said:

"You look more lovely than I have time to tell you, but remind me not to forget to do so to-morrow morning."

His words awakened Athena very effectively; for she could not help wondering where they would be to-morrow and what would happen between now and then.

When they had arrived back at the Taverna all the guests had gone and everything was very quiet.

She knew then that Orion had made plans and that she must come back from the heights of ecstasy to face reality.

"I shall have to tell him the truth sooner or later," she told herself.

Then because she knew she was afraid that it might in some way spoil their happiness she shied away from that moment like a horse frightened by a shadow on the road.

But Orion was already dressed in the clothes in which she had first seen him, and when he left the room Athena rose.

She realised with a sudden depression that she would have to put on the gown of which she had been so ashamed and which Nonika had saved her from having to wear as her wedding gown.

However there was no time to worry about such details. Orion was waiting downstairs and she knew how it infuriated her father if he was ever kept waiting by his womenfolk.

She washed and tried not to think of how unbelievably wonderful and perfect everything had been the night before.

There would be time later to remember, to recall the ecstasy she had found with her husband, and he with her.

Now she must try to be practical.

Nonika's beautiful wedding-gown was lying on a chair and Athena turned to the cupboard, expecting to find her own gown hanging there, but the cupboard was empty.

Even as she thought she must call down the stairs and ask for it, there was a knock on the door and Madame Argeros came in carrying her gown followed by Nonika.

"Good-morning," Madame Argeros said. "You must hurry, for your husband has already started his breakfast and he tells me you have a long way to go."

"I am nearly..." Athena began, then broke off.

She looked at her gown which Madame Argeros was carrying, and realised that it had been washed and pressed and looked almost as fresh as it had been when she had first put it on, what now seemed a century ago, in the Palace.

"You have washed my gown!" she exclaimed. "Oh, Madame Argeros, it must have taken you half the night! How can I ever thank you?"

"I could not have you leaving us in such a state," Madame Argeros said, "especially as it was through no fault of your own that your dress was dirtied."

"But you have done it so beautifully," Athena cried.

The gown had in fact been exquisitely laundered as the Greek women wash their own blouses and their men's shirts.

It glowed with a whiteness that seemed to reflect the sunshine.

As Athena slipped it on she thought with delight that now she would not be ashamed for Orion to see her.

"You have been so kind – so very kind," she said to Nonika, because Madame had already hurried down the stairs.

"We are glad we could be of help to Orion's wife," Nonika replied.

"You have been more than that," Athena said. "I felt like a real bride in your beautiful gown, and it has brought me so much happiness that I know it will do the same for you."

"I hope so," Nonika smiled.

"And as a wedding present," Athena went on, choosing her words with care, "I hope you will allow me to send you a part of your trousseau. I thought perhaps you would like some nightgowns like mine, and perhaps some petticoats and other garments made of the same material."

She saw Nonika's eyes widen in sheer astonishment. Then the Greek girl said stammeringly:

"D .. do you really ... mean that? I thought your nightgown so ... pretty that I might try to ... copy it."

"I will send you a dozen," Athena said. "In the meantime keep this one if it is any use to you as a pattern."

Nonika drew in her breath, then she said:

"It is too kind ... too generous. Perhaps I should not ... take such a gift."

"I should be very hurt and disappointed if you refused," Athena replied. "After all, you lent me something of such inestimable value, which could never be calculated in any currency except that of friendship."

She smiled as she went on:

"We are friends, Nonika, and that is what I hope we shall be all our lives. Nothing is too good or too precious to give in return for friendship."

"You are right," Nonika said, "and I can only say thank you."

She paused, then she said as if it was impossible to suppress the words:

"You will not . . . forget?"

"No, I promise, I shall not forget," Athena laughed.

She put her arms round Nonika's shoulders and kissed her; then picking up her bonnet she ran down the stairs, eager to be with Orion again.

There were so many good-byes to say when they had hastily eaten their breakfast that it was only when they were outside that Athena looked at the horse she was to ride, expecting it to be the one belonging to Spiros.

But she found it was in fact a very different animal which awaited her.

Although it did not equal the well-bred qualities of Orion's stallion, it was obviously a horse capable both of endurance and of speed.

Athena looked questioningly at Orion and he explained with a smile:

"Your first wedding-present, my darling. I bought it for you this morning. It is the best the village can provide."

"I am delighted with it," Athena answered.

"At least it will carry you where we have to go," he said, "and you have not yet told me where that is."

Her eyes widened and she laughed.

"I know it cannot be far," he went on, "because you came to the Port of Itea."

"It is ridiculous how little we know about each other," she said.

"On the contrary," he replied. "I know everything about you, everything that is important, and to me our love is a miracle!"

She blushed at the passion in his voice and her eyes fell before his.

They were talking in English so that no-one else could

understand. Then she said, having already decided what to say:

"I am staying at Mikis."

"At the Hotel Poseidon, I suppose?" he said. "It is a favourite spot for tourists, but I thought you were more likely to be at Ossios."

"Mikis is nearer," Athena replied, realising that Ossios was on the opposite shore to the promontory on which the Palace was built.

Orion helped her onto her horse, arranged her full skirts over the pummel and said a little anxiously:

"Do you think you will be comfortable? We have a long way to go."

"I am used to riding," she answered, "and I seldom find it tiring."

"That is what I thought you would say."

"How did you know I could ride?"

"I knew you would ride superbly well, like everything else you do," he answered, and she smiled from sheer happiness.

He swung himself onto the stallion's back who was behaving in his usual obstreperous manner. Then amid the cheers of the crowds who had come to see them off they rode down and along the first part of the thirty mile road which led eventually to Thebes.

After they had left Delphi behind there was a long and lonely descent from the mountainside.

Athena stopped and drew her horse to a standstill as Orion suggested she should look back.

Now she could see almost the whole range of the Parnassus mountains and there was snow on the tops of some of them, gleaming dazzlingly in the sunlight, and there was also a superb view over Delphi itself.

"I hate to say good-bye," Athena said in a low voice.

"It is only *au revoir*," Orion replied. "We will come back perhaps every year to celebrate, and in the years to come we will bring our children, and I shall show them where I found a goddess asleep amongst the ruins of her own Temple."

Athena's eyes met his and he said hoarsely:

"If you look at me like that I shall have to kiss you and that means we shall never reach our destination."

"Do we ... have to go ... back?" Athena asked.

There was a little pause before he replied:

"I cannot help feeling that your relatives must be getting worried by now, unless you gave them a very good explanation for your disappearance. We would not wish them to send out a search-party looking for you."

"No, of course not!" Athena exclaimed.

"Leave everything to me, my darling," Orion said. "I promise you I will sort it out with the minimum of difficulty and trouble. Do you trust me?"

"You know I do."

"Then let us go on," he said. "The sooner we are free of all such tiresome obligations, the sooner we can think of ourselves, which means that I can think of you."

As if his words spurred them on they set off at a sharp pace and after proceeding for some miles they left the main road to begin what Athena knew was the descent which would lead them eventually to the sea and Mikis.

The land was very undulating and it was impossible to ride direct since they had to take various detours to avoid the hill-tops.

But away from the heights of Delphi the flowers intensified in beauty and the blossom was richer on the trees, and it also grew a great deal hotter.

Athena was glad after all that she had worn her bonnet for the journey, because the sun would have been too hot on her head. She hoped that her white skin would not be sun-burnt, even though she thought that the brown of Orion's bare neck and arms was exceedingly becoming to him.

About eleven o'clock they stopped in the shade of some trees to eat the luncheon with which Madame Argeros had provided them.

"I thought it would be more fun for us to be alone," Orion said, "than to eat in some small Taverna where doubtless the food would be indifferent and the wine flavoured with resin, which you would not like."

"I am feeling hungry even though it may be unromantic," Athena smiled.

"Then suppose you unpack what there is to eat, while I cool the wine in that small cascade," he suggested.

Athena followed the direction of his eyes and saw a waterfall in a ravine near where they had stopped.

He walked away towards it, having given her some packages from his saddle-bag.

Athena opened them to find as she expected that Madame Argeros, despite the earliness of their departure, had cooked them a whole lot of delicious Greek specialities that would have tempted the appetite of anyone far less hungry than they were.

She was not certain what all the things were although she recognised *dolmades* which were vine-leaves folded over mince-meat and rice.

But whatever was provided Orion was prepared to eat it, and he lay on the ground beside her and somehow there was no need to talk because they were so happy.

Only when they had finished nearly everything that Madame Argeros provided for them and Orion was drinking the last of the wine, did Athena realise that now was the moment when she should tell him about herself.

"What are you thinking about?" he asked unexpectedly.

"You," she replied.

"That is the right answer, my darling, you should always be thinking of me, as I am thinking about you."

"What were you thinking about me?" Athena asked.

"I was thinking how much I love you," he answered, "and

how fortunate I am – the luckiest man in the world – to have found you."

"That is what I feel about you."

"We think the same, we feel the same, we are the same," he said softly.

He stretched out his arms.

"Come here!"

It was a command and for one moment Athena hesitated. Then she knew that she wanted the touch of his lips so urgently, so insistently, that she could not wait.

What was the point of talking when they could be kissing? Why should she spoil this moment with what might prove to be unpleasant information?

She moved swiftly towards him, and close in his arms it was impossible to think of anything else but him.

* * *

When they rode on there was a flush on Athena's cheeks and she felt warm and weak with sheer happiness.

She did not wish to make decisions, she did not wish to force herself to choose the right moment in which to make revelations about herself to Orion.

She only wanted to know that she was loved.

She loved him so overwhelmingly that she was afraid, as she had never been afraid in her whole life, that her happiness was only a glorious iridescent bubble and it might burst if it was roughly handled.

"I adore you!" Orion said as he lifted her into the saddle and that was all she wanted to think about as she rode along beside him.

They had come a long way since the morning, and two hours later, in the distance Athena had her first glimpse of the blue of the Gulf of Corinth.

It was still a long way ahead but growing nearer all the time, and when suddenly they dropped down to sea level she realised with a frightened leap of her heart that she had still not said what must be said.

"Are we far from Mikis now?" she asked in a small voice.

"Only about a mile or so," Orion replied. "You are not too tired, my darling? It has been a long way, but you have ridden magnificently and it was really much easier than if we had come by sea. If we had done that I would not have known what to do with my horse."

"We could hardly put him in the boat," Athena smiled, "or make him swim behind us."

Orion laughed.

"That is what I thought."

"Orion ..." she began in a tremulous little tone, but he did not seem to hear her because he said:

"I have decided what we will do. I will leave you at the Hotel and as now it is getting on for two o'clock I suggest you follow everyone else's example and have a siesta.

"When the whole world stirs again at about four you can tell your relations that you are married and that I shall be arriving at six. You can then introduce me and explanations can be made on either side."

He smiled as he added:

"I do not think they will be too angry with you, my precious. I promise that I will give a good account of myself."

"I am ... sure you ... will ... but ..." Athena began.

Again what she was about to say was lost because Orion had spurred his horse and they were moving more quickly than they had moved before over a piece of flat grassland to where in the distance there were the roofs and the dome of the Church in the small Harbour of Mikis.

"I will have to tell him later," she thought and hurried her own horse forward to catch up with him.

Orion drew his stallion to a standstill when they were within a hundred yards of the Hotel Poseidon which stood above the town looking down on the harbour.

It was quite an impressive looking building and had, Athena thought, only recently been built.

One of the results of a united Constitution and peace within the country was that visitors were now flocking back to Greece and there was every likelihood that the tourist trade would bring the Government the foreign currency they needed so badly to balance their economy.

"I am going to leave you now, my precious," Orion said. "Go straight to the Hotel and, if you can have a rest before you become involved in explanations for your absence, so much the better."

He paused then added:

"I will come to you at six o'clock. Do not be worried or upset in the meantime. There is no need for it — that I promise you!"

"You will not ... forget?" she asked, as Nonika had done.

"That would be impossible, Heart of my Heart!"

He put out his hand and she laid her fingers in it.

"I love you, my darling," he said. "I love you, completely and overwhelmingly, and I swear to you that never again will we be parted for a single moment. We will be together and nothing and nobody shall come between us."

"You are ... sure of ... that?" Athena asked in sudden fear.

"Trust me."

"I do trust you."

He raised her fingers to his lips. Then as if he had no wish to say more he moved his horse.

"Go straight to the Hotel, my precious," he said. "I shall watch until you are safely there so that nothing can happen to you when my back is turned."

"I will be ... all right."

Athena smiled at him and rode off conscious that he was watching her.

As she went she decided she would have to go to the Hotel to make quite certain he did not see her ride up the twisting road towards the Palace.

When she reached the Hotel entrance she looked back. Although there was no sign of Orion she could not be certain that he was not watching her from the hillside, so she dismounted and went inside.

Having told a groom to hold her horse for a few minutes she ordered herself a glass of lemonade.

When she had drunk a little of it she paid the waiter who seemed to be half asleep and resentful at having to attend to her when he might be dozing, and went outside.

The groom helped her back into the saddle.

She was certain that by now Orion would no longer be watching for her but had gone to his own home, wherever it was in the vicinity.

Although it was only two o'clock, she felt there was a lot to do before she must be back in the Hotel to meet Orion at six. So she forced her horse as fast as possible up the road to the Palace.

It did not take long and as she rode in past the sentries she thought how lovely the building looked, gleaming white against the mountainside, its garden a riot of colour with two fountains playing on the green lawns.

But she was no longer interested in the Palace and intent only on planning exactly how she should behave once she was inside it.

As she had expected, everything was very quiet and there were only a few junior servants on duty who did not seem in the least surprised at her appearance.

Without making any explanations as to why she had returned she merely told the senior amongst them to inform Lady Beatrice Wade when the siesta was over that Lady Mary was in her bed-room.

The servant bowed and Athena knew that he would obey her orders and would not think of disturbing her Aunt for at least two and a half hours.

Then she went upstairs and once inside her own room rang for her maid.

Because she wished to obey Orion she undressed and got into bed.

"Call me at four o'clock," she told the maid, "when I would like a bath."

Athena realised as she spoke that she was almost too tired to say the words and literally as her head touched the pillow she fell asleep.

* * *

She awoke to realise that she had been dreaming of the sound of rushing water that came from the Castalian spring, but it was in fact her bath being prepared next door.

The bathrooms in the Palace had been designed in the Roman manner, sunk deep into the floor and Athena thought there was something very attractive in stepping down into her bath and sitting with the cool water reflecting the tiles which had been copied from some of the ancient Roman Villas.

The thought of bathing got her out of bed, and only when she had washed and was drying herself with the big white Turkish towel did she begin to think apprehensively of what she must say to her Aunt and even more important the explanation she must make to the Prince.

It was not going to be easy – she was aware of that – and what frightened her more than anything else was that the Prince might try to denounce Orion as a "fortune-hunter".

It was a thought that had lain at the back of her mind and now the idea forced itself upon her.

"It is so obvious that to discredit him they will say that he must have known all along who I am and married me so hastily to make quite certain that my money became his.

"How could anyone think such things of Orion?" Athena asked indignantly.

But she knew it was because she had come back from the sacred peace and serenity of Delphi to the world where people's minds were suspicious and bad motives were easier to believe than good.

"Orion will answer for himself," she thought proudly.

At the same time she knew that she was a coward because she was afraid.

Her maid was waiting for her in the bed-room and as she put on the beautiful lace-trimmed underclothes like those she had promised to Nonika for her trousseau Athena was thinking deeply.

She was dressed as far as her petticoats and was arranging her hair in the mirror when the door was flung open and Lady Beatrice came into the room.

"Mary!" she exclaimed. "I have just learned that you have returned! How could you go away in such an irresponsible manner without even leaving an address?"

"I am sorry, Aunt Beatrice," Athena said rising, "but..."

"I dare say you have a good explanation," Lady Beatrice interrupted, "but I have no time to hear it now. All I can say is that I consider it extremely thoughtless of you."

"I am sorry," Athena began again.

"You will have to tell me all about it later," Lady Beatrice added. "But hurry now and put on your best gown and make yourself look presentable."

"Why?" Athena asked in surprise.

"Why?" Lady Beatrice echoed. "Because the Prince is here! Luckily I shall not have to make any explanation for your absence. That would have been embarrassing, to say the least of it."

"The ... Prince is ... here?" Athena repeated almost stupidly.

"Yes, at last!" Lady Beatrice said. "Goodness knows, we have been waiting for him long enough! Now come along, Mary. There is no point in keeping him waiting, despite the manner in which he has behaved to us."

She hurried across the room as she spoke to pull open the wardrobe doors.

"You had better put on your blue grenadine," she said. "That is the gown your grandmother thought you should wear when you first met him. It is certainly one of the most becoming creations we have brought with us."

"Y..yes ... I will wear the blue," Athena said.

She was thinking as she spoke that it did not matter what the Prince thought, but she would like Orion to see her in the blue grenadine.

It was a very elaborate gown with a huge skirt of wide frills each one trimmed at the edge with real lace. It had the very becoming off-the-shoulder, boat-shaped neckline which had been made so fashionable by Queen Victoria.

"No jewellery, I think – no – perhaps your pearls," Lady Beatrice was saying. "You do not want to look ostentatious. At the same time it is important that he should admire you."

"Aunt Beatrice ... I have something to tell you ..." Athena began hesitatingly.

She knew the maid who was doing up her gown could not understand English, and she felt she must tell her Aunt now what she was going to say when she met the Prince.

"You can tell me later, Mary," Lady Beatrice said quickly. "There is really no time now. Just hurry! I know Colonel Stefanatis is waiting for us in the hall."

There was nothing Athena could do but clasp the pearls round her neck, slip her lace mittens over her hands and pick up a handkerchief.

"Come along! Come along!" Lady Beatrice was saying impatiently. "First impressions are very important, as I have told you often enough, and to be late is always inexcusable."

She went ahead of Athena down the stairs at such a pace that her niece almost had to run to keep up with her.

When they reached the hall Colonel Stefanatis bowed to Lady Beatrice, then to Athena, giving her at the same time a look that she thought was both curious and reproachful.

She was quite sure that he had worried over her disappearance perhaps more than her Aunt had done.

"This way, ladies, please," he said in his most pompous manner.

He led the way down a broad corridor towards a room which Athena knew she had hitherto not seen.

'How shall I ... begin?' she thought frantically. 'What shall I ... say?'

She wondered if it would be easier to speak to the Prince in English or Greek, and she decided that having greeted him she would ask if she could speak to him alone.

Everybody would think it very forward and unconventional but after all what did it matter?

They were moving through a part of the Palace which she thought must be exclusively the Prince's because now there were sporting pictures on the walls, ancient guns and several portraits.

There was one which she felt sure must be the Prince himself as it was of a young man with a short dark beard.

She would have liked to stop to look at it and prepare herself for the man she was to meet. But her Aunt and the Colonel were walking so quickly that she could only give the picture a cursory glance as she was forced to keep up with them.

Ahead she saw two liveried servants, one on either side of a pair of mahogany doors and the Colonel looked back to make sure that she was still there.

Then the doors were opened and he stepped through them.

Athena drew a deep breath.

"Lady Beatrice Wade, Your Highness," she heard Colonel Stefanitis announce, "and Lady Mary Wade!"

Athena realised that her heart was beating violently in her breast.

'There is no need to be frightened,' she thought, 'Orion will look after me! Help me, oh my darling, help me to be brave!'

She said his name over and over to herself as if it was a talisman.

She realised that her Aunt was curtseying in front of her and heard a man's voice say:

"You must forgive me, Lady Beatrice. I am more apologetic than I can possibly convey that I have been delayed and that you should have arrived here sooner than I expected."

Athena raised her eyes.

Somehow the voice seemed curiously familiar.

Then she saw standing at her Aunt's side raising her gloved hand perfunctorily to his lips was a man wearing a white uniform coat with gold epaulettes.

For a moment it was difficult to focus her eyes, until as he straightened himself after bowing over her Aunt's hand he turned to face her and the whole world seemed to stand still.

It was impossible to think – impossible to breathe and it seemed as if he too had been turned to stone.

Then as their eyes met it was as if they reached out and touched each other and everybody and everything else vanished.

"Athena my precious!" Orion exclaimed. "What are you doing here?"

Chapter Seven

Athena walked out onto the balcony and stood looking at the last glimmer of the sun as it sank into the blue of the sea.

It turned the hills and the coastline to every kind of gold; gold fading to russet brown, gold shot through with black, green and purple in the fading light.

And the gold patterns on the sea shimmered against the golden outline of the shore.

She leant over the balustrade thinking she had not seen this view of the sea from the room she had previously occupied in the Palace.

Now she was in the Prince's Suite and the room behind her was so magnificent and at the same time so artistically beautiful that she felt as if it belonged to a fairy-tale.

But then nothing had seemed real, nothing since that moment when she discovered that Orion was the Prince, and regardless of everybody else in the room he had held her close in his arms and she had known that she need no longer be afraid.

They had dined very early because he had thought she must be tired, and now her maids had arrayed her in one of the lovely gauze negligées which she had brought from London in her trousseau.

It barely concealed the curves of her figure as she stood staring at the last glimpse of Apollo before he vanished into the sable of the night.

She heard a footstep behind her but she did not turn her head, and after a moment's pause Orion came and stood beside her.

It was the first time they had been alone since he had

left her early in the afternoon to go to the Hotel Poseidon.

He did not speak, but she knew his eyes were on her face and after a moment she said:

"How ... could I have known ... how could I have even suspected for ... one moment that you might be the ... Prince? I was told he had a beard."

"A beard can prove to be a very effective disguise," he said with laughter in his voice, "but to remove it can be equally effective."

"You have done that before?"

"Several times when I wanted to go to Delphi," he admitted. "It was fascinating the way I could walk out of the Palace and nobody gave me a second glance."

There was a moment's silence, before she said:

"Colonel Stefanatis ... looked for ... you at the ... Villa of ... Madame Helena."

She thought Orion might stiffen at the name, but instead he leant over the balustrade beside her and said:

"How do you know that?"

"The Colonel did not realise that I could speak Greek," Athena answered, "and I ... overheard what he was saying to the officer who had been looking for you."

"Do you want me to explain?"

"No."

It was the truth, Athena thought. There were really no explanations needed between them.

Of course there had been women in his life before they met, but she knew now without his telling her that if they had mattered to him once they were pale shadows beside what he felt for her.

"Then I will tell you," he said with a faint smile. "The affection I had for Helena, who is an extremely intelligent and cultured woman, was over before I reluctantly accepted the suggestion that for the sake of my people I should marry an English heiress."

He paused, then added:

"I was not hiding in her Villa for the simple reason that

she is leaving Greece and building a house for herself in the South of France."

Athena did not speak and after a moment he said:

"If you were surprised at learning my identity, how do you think I could have imagined that the cold-blooded, stiff, awe-inspiring heiress from England should prove to be my own little goddess, warm, loving and with a fire within her which echoes the fire in me?"

Athena felt herself tremble at the passion in his words. Then he asked:

"Why did you not tell me?"

"I ... meant to," Athena said, "I tried to when we were having luncheon together ... but then you ... kissed me and nothing else ... seemed to matter."

"Nothing else ever will matter."

He did not touch her but moved a little nearer to her before he said:

"I went to Delphi because at the last moment I panicked into thinking that even to help my poor people – and they are very poor – I could not saddle myself with a woman I did not love."

Athena turned to look at him.

"I went there for the same ... reason. When I came to Greece I expected the Prince would be a man like you but I was terrified when I met the gossiping, pleasure-seeking Courtiers at the Palace in Athens."

"I loathe the place – that is why I never go there."

"You are not ... angry with me for having ... kept my secret? I was preparing to tell the Prince I could not marry him ... and the thought that ... Orion was waiting for me ... gave me the courage to do so."

"I am still waiting, my darling."

She looked in his eyes and made a little movement as if she would go closer to him. But then she said:

"Our marriage is ... legal? We will not have to be married again?"

"It is completely legal," he replied, "and I know that like me you could not bear to repeat what to both of us was an unforgettable experience."

"I loved becoming your ... wife in that dear little Church with only the ... people who ... love you present," Athena said in a low voice.

"I have learnt from your Aunt that you were christened 'Athena Mayville'," Orion said, "and Count Theodoros is actually one of my titles."

"Then I am really your wife!"

"Do you want me to prove it?"

He would have taken her in his arms but with a faint gesture Athena stopped him.

"I want you to know one thing," she said. "Even if you had been quite poor and of no social consequence, I would still have been happy ... wildly, crazily happy with you ... even if you refused to touch my money."

"You anticipated that I might do that?"

Athena looked away from him a little shyly.

"I was sure you were very proud," she said, "and I was afraid that the Prince might ... revenge himself on you in ... some manner, in which case we should have been obliged to use my fortune to leave Greece! Otherwise I anticipated that you might feel it a ... humiliation to live on your wife's ... wealth."

"You would have cooked for me and looked after me?" Orion asked.

"I would have tried to be as good a cook as Madame Argeros," Athena answered.

Orion gave a laugh of sheer happiness.

"My darling! Was there ever anyone like you?" he asked. "I said you were perfect, but there are degrees of perfection of which even I was not aware. You are everything Athena should be."

He touched her cheek with his hand as he went on:

"You have her beauty, her clear-sighted intelligence and,

having put her armour away, like her you cultivate the feminine graces and of course the olive groves."

He was half-serious, half-teasing, and now Athena moved close against him.

"Shall we cultivate the ... olive-groves together?" she whispered.

His arms went round her and his lips were on her hair as he said:

"There are so many things I want to do with you and as the goddess of wisdom I know that you will guide, inspire and help my people – they need you desperately!"

"And ... you?" Athena enquired.

He looked down at her, his eyes searching her face as he said:

"I cannot live without you – does that answer your question?"

"I love you, Orion! I love you and I am afraid that ... this is a ... dream from which we might both ... awaken."

"It is a dream that will stay with us all the days of our lives," he answered, "and every moment, every second that I am with you, my darling little goddess, I fall more deeply, more overwhelmingly in love."

He felt a quiver run through her at his words and his arms tightened around the softness of her body which seemed to melt into his.

The last golden finger of the sun touched them both and illuminated them with a golden aura.

Orion looked down into Athena's eyes shining in the light that came not only from the sun but also from the glory within herself.

"You are tired, my precious," he said, "but if you look at me like that it will be hard for me to let you rest and not make love to you as I want to do."

"I ... want your love," Athena said. "I want to make sure that I am really your ... wife and that I need no longer be afraid of ... losing you."

"You will never do that," he answered, "and I think you realise as I do, my dearest love, that we have been joined together not only by the Church but also by the power of Apollo and Athena goddess of love."

He paused and his voice deepened as he said:

"I believe with all my heart that they brought us together. We were meant for each other since the beginning of time, and an instinct which was part of the divine took us both to Delphi."

"I think that too," Athena said. "In fact I am sure of it."

"Fate moved in strange ways, and there is always a pattern behind everything," Orion went on. "There is a reason for us meeting and loving each other, which will affect the lives and the future of all those with whom we come in contact."

"You mean that ... together we can do something for ... Greece?" Athena asked.

"Nothing ever really happens by chance, and nothing is ever wasted," Orion replied. "That is why, my darling, there are gods who plan our destiny."

"As long as I am with you," Athena whispered, "and as long as we can do what is right and good ... that is all I ask of the future."

She had been moved by the solemnity of his tone, and now he turned towards the sea and the mountains in the distance, which were bathed in the pale transparent limpid grey of the dusk.

"Once this country gave to the world the power to think," he said quietly. "Men's minds moved quicker here and their hearts were lifted in a manner which has never been forgotten."

He paused before he continued:

"That should be the goal of all Greeks to-day, to find again the vision of perfect beauty and of clear thinking which was our contribution to the world."

There was a radiance in Orion's expression and his voice seemed to have a special vibrance as he said:

"Once the Greeks saw holiness wherever they walked and they translated it into beauty."

Athena thought of Delphi and of the Parthenon, and understood what he was trying to say, as he went on:

"That holiness and beauty must come again for it has been too long from the earth. That is the ideal, my darling, to which we in our way must dedicate ourselves."

"I will do that ... if you will ... help me," Athena said.

"We will do it together," he answered. "You and I will try to find the light of the gods and bring it to those who need it desperately."

As he spoke the grey of the sky deepened to sable and the mystery of the darkening night enfolded them.

And yet it seemed to Athena that some light within themselves remained. It came from their hearts and was in fact some of the splendour that had once belonged to Greece.

Because she was a little over-awed and at the same time deeply moved by the way Orion had spoken, she moved closer to him as if for protection, half afraid of the greatness of his vision and all he asked of her.

Because he understood he held her very close and his lips were against the softness of her cheek.

"Such ideals lie in our souls and cannot be shown to ordinary people because they would not understand," he said quietly, "but our love and happiness in each other is different."

His mouth moved over her skin before he went on:

"I believe that, in itself, will bring happiness to others, as you, my beautiful one, gave happiness yesterday to the simple friends I have in Delphi."

"They have no idea who you are?" Athena asked.

"To them I am Orion, someone they love because I love them. I like to keep it that way so that there is always somewhere I can go and just be myself, and there are no demands made on me except as a man."

"I love you as a ... man," Athena said, her voice deepening on the word, "but I also love you as Orion and last night when you ... made me your ... wife I thought that the ... constellation of stars shone ... around you."

"We were enchanted," he said, "and I think that the light of Apollo brought us both an ecstasy that is only given to those favoured by the gods."

His lips found her mouth.

At first it was a kiss without passion, but something more perfect, more sacred, like the moonlight on the Sanctuary at Delphi.

Then the closeness of him and his lips awakened the fire that had burnt within Athena the night before and she felt it rise in him.

They clung together feeling the flames of love uniting their bodies and exciting their minds.

"I love you! I love you, Orion," Athena whispered.

Now his kiss became more demanding, fiercely, insistently passionate and with it an exaltation and a rapture which made her feel that once again he would carry her up into the sky until they reached the stars that were just appearing in the velvet darkness above them.

Then with his lips on hers, and holding her close against his throbbing heart, both of them aware of the urgency of their need for each other, Orion drew Athena from the balcony and into the room behind them.

On the sea the reflection of light from the rising moon touched the softly moving waves with silver as if they caressed the body of the goddess of love.

Other books by Barbara Cartland

Romantic Novels, over 150, the most recently published being:

The Husband Hunters
The Blue-Eyed Witch
A Dream from the Night
Never Laugh at Love
The Secret of the Glen
The Proud Princess
Hungry for Love
The Heart Triumphant
The Disgraceful Duke
Vote for Love
The Mysterious Maid-Servant
The Magic of Love

Autobiographical and Biographical

The Isthmus Years   1919–1939
The Years of Opportunity   1939–1945
I Search for Rainbows   1945–1966
We Danced All Night   1919–1929
Ronald Cartland (with a foreword by Sir Winston Churchill)
Polly, My Wonderful Mother

Historical

Bewitching Women
The Outrageous Queen (The Story of Queen Christina of Sweden)
The Scandalous Life of King Carol
The Private Life of King Charles II
The Private Life of Elizabeth, Empress of Austria
Diane de Poitiers
Metternich – the Passionate Diplomat

Sociology
You in the Home
The Fascinating Forties
Marriage for Moderns
Be Vivid, Be Vital
Love, Life and Sex
Vitamins for Vitality
Husbands and Wives
Etiquette
The Many Facets of Love
Sex and the Teenager
The Book of Charm
Living Together
The Youth Secret
The Magic of Honey
Barbara Cartland's Book of Beauty and Health
Men are Wonderful

Cookery
Barbara Cartland's Health Food Cookery Book
Food for Love
Magic of Honey Cookbook

Editor of
The Common Problems by Ronald Cartland
(with a preface by the Rt. Hon. The Earl of Selborne, P.C.)

Drama
Blood Money
French Dressing

Philosophy
Touch the Stars

Radio Operetta
The Rose and the Violet (Music by Mark Lubbock)
Performed in 1942

Radio Plays
The Caged Bird: An episode in the Life of Elizabeth, Empress of Austria
Performed in 1957

Verse
Lines on Life and Love

Barbara Cartland
Love Locked In 50p

Syrilla first fell in love with Aristide when she was nine – though they had never met . . . Now she is eighteen and the Duc thirty, and she is overjoyed to learn that a marriage has been arranged between them. Living quietly in the country with her father, she is unaware that Aristide's scandalous exploits in Paris have made his name a byword for debauchery . . .

The Magic of Love 50p

Melita Cranleigh arrives in Martinique to begin a new life as a governess – she is apprehensive of the future, and afraid of what her new employer will be like. Etienne, Comte de Vesonne, proves to be young and distinguished; and Melita's life soon resembles an exciting dream as she and Etienne are drawn together irresistibly – while the drums beat out their primitive message, and the rituals of Voodoo cast a dark shadow over slaves and plantation alike. . .

The Taming of Lady Lorinda 50p

When Durstan Hayle first set eyes on Lorinda Camborne, the toast of St James's, she was circling the ballroom on a black horse, apparently naked except for the red-gold hair that completed her ensemble as Lady Godiva. Incensed by her behaviour, Durstan wagers a thousand guineas that he can tame this headstrong, unpredictable beauty . . .

You can buy these and other Barbara Cartland books from booksellers and newsagents; or direct from the following address:
Pan Books, Cavaye Place, London SW10 9PG
Send purchase price plus 15p for the first book and 5p for
each additional book, to allow for postage and packing
Prices quoted are applicable in UK

While every effort is made to keep prices low, it is sometimes necessary to increase prices at short notice. Pan Books reserve the right to show on covers new retail prices which may differ from those advertised in the text or elsewhere